THE RABBI WHO PRAYED WITH FIRE

A
RABBI VIVIAN
MYSTERY

RACHEL SHARONA LEWIS

Rachel Sharona Lewis
Watertown, MA
rachielew@gmail.com

ISBN: 978-1-7923-5652-0
Ebook ISBN: 978-1-7923-5653-7

Book design and composition by Brian Phillips Design
Cover design by Brian Phillips Design
Edited by Anna Schnur-Fishman

First Edition

Printed in the United States of America

for my mom,
and first rabbi, Sunnie

PROLOGUE

AMID THE CROWD of bewildered congregants gathering outside the synagogue, Vivian could feel the unsteadiness in the air. The wail of the approaching fire trucks was getting louder. She searched for words: words of closure for the unfinished Shabbat prayers, words that would soothe her congregants, words that could reassure the two unfamiliar millennials in attendance that this was *not* what Friday night services normally entailed.

But there were no words. Amid the chaos, the screams, the sirens, and now the streams of water unleashed onto the flames, Vivian could only summon tears. She surveyed her flock and noted with relief that none seemed to have sustained serious injuries upon their rushed exodus from the sanctuary. The verse they'd cut short still hung in the air: "Come, my beloved, to meet the Sabbath bride."

Tears dripped from her face onto the velvet dressing of the Torah to which she held fast. *This Torah must have been through so much*, she thought, as it brushed against her ear. *What can it tell me?*

Oddly, the only congregant's voice that Vivian was able to decipher from the noise swirling around her did not sound fearful or in need of comfort. As Vivian stared ahead at the advancing blaze, she heard the unmistakable raspy chuckle of elderly Philip Katz.

"Now that's one smokin' Shabbos bride."

ONE

Rabbi Joseph Glass scanned the sanctuary. Years of congregational work had made him skilled at counting, sorting. Board members. Those whose homes he considered kosher enough to eat in. Pregnant women. People over sixty-five. People between forty-five and sixty-five. Thirty-five and forty-five. And small children. Never anyone between eighteen and thirty-five, save the kids visiting from college.

On a cool Shabbat day in the middle of Passover, he counted thirty-two between forty-five and sixty-five; forty-four above sixty-five; and a few out-of-towners who did not look younger than forty, though Joseph could not say for sure. No one younger.

Despite the consistent encouragement, the signs, and the greeter's invitation for people to sit toward the front, those in attendance scattered themselves throughout the faded maroon hall, built a century ago to accommodate six hundred. Whole rows of the wooden chairs, fastened together ten across, remained empty. The morning light angled toward them as if to rub it in.

Joseph approached the bima, his trembling hands imperceptible to the rest of the congregation. Even after thirty-six years as a congregational rabbi, he still grew nervous in the moments right before a sermon.

"Shabbat shalom," he began. "This morning, I want to talk about the four children that we encountered at our seders this past week, one child in particular. We spend a lot of time condemning the *rasha*, the Wicked Son"—wagging his pointer finger, he glanced down at his notes—"I mean, the Wicked Child, whose question 'What is this tradition to you?' is interpreted as an absolution of responsibility and belonging to the Jewish people. We also give ample attention to the *chacham*, the Wise Son—the Wise Child, that is—who affirms Jewish experience and practice, who follows the rules laid out before him and meets high expectations. Ready to learn, he says, 'Teach me your ways, teach me *our* ways.' We gravitate toward the extremes, toward the children who exist in clear categories, toward the ones we know how to respond to. Those we condemn or extol.

"We pay less attention to those in the middle, those who it's more difficult to answer. I want to focus on the Child Who Doesn't Know How to Ask, the one who doesn't know how to enter the conversation. Because in our current Jewish world, the statistics show that many of our children fall into this middle space. And those numbers are growing.

"A lot of ink has been spilled, or should I say keyboards rubbed off, speculating about where the millennials are. Why don't they come to shul? Why don't they pay for important services and institutions? Why don't they respect who and what has come before them and see the meaning of what we have sustained? What will happen to our people if they stay away? Many of you have wondered this aloud to me about your own children, as they chart their paths forward in life."

Joseph locked eyes with Ezra Abrams, who had come into his office the previous week to mourn his daughter's choice to marry a Hindu man she met while teaching English abroad. For a moment the faces of his own children, Jake and Naomi, flashed in his mind.

He fingered through his notes for his next line. "The explanations about the different children's questions arise from a predetermined conversation about the exact way things are done on Passover. The tradition, the elders, the parents set the terms of the discussion and expect the children to follow suit. We build structures and expect them to walk right in. Older generations disappear hoping future ones will follow in their footsteps.

"But times have changed. The world is messier, more complicated. Kids have more choices of who they can be. We give them mixed messages. Follow this path. Be your true self. But younger generations have so many paths laid out before them, so many possible true selves they could be."

Joseph straightened his kippah. "Passover is customarily a time for children to ask questions, presumably with parents answering. Well, perhaps this year, we can ask questions to our children, knowing that, perhaps, they are the ones with the answers. 'My child, what does this tradition mean to you?'"

He glanced at Rabbi Vivian Green, adjusting in the chair to his left. Vivian, the assistant rabbi the community had hired a year earlier with the hope of attracting more young people, often seemed uncomfortable sitting in the plush chairs reserved for leadership—as if she were a child anticipating the end of class.

It was Vivian who had inspired this particular sermon. As they prepared for the congregation-wide seder, she had continued to draw his attention to the two sons ("the two *children*," she would say), the ones who did not live on the extremes, but perhaps just needed to be asked different questions, better questions. Or perhaps offered some silence that they themselves could be trusted to fill in. Then, maybe, they could set the terms of the conversation.

The exchange stuck with Joseph, and when he sat down to write his sermon, he was too tired to come up with something new. So, he had elaborated upon Vivian's prompt.

"The generation of Israelites that witnessed God's miracles of liberation," Joseph continued, "was not the same generation that entered the promised land. The latter had fresh eyes and strength, they were not broken down by the indignities and suffering of slavery. They could fight for and build a new world, a better one.

"The children who do not know how to ask still have the capacity to be our teachers, if we listen for the conversations that they want to have, if we become familiar with the world they want to build and live in. Perhaps they hold the key to the future they will carry forward far beyond many of us."

Joseph's voice did not slowly deepen as he stated the last words, as it usually did, in order to indicate the sermon's end. Rather, they came out higher and abrupt, as if the last sentence were a question.

Casting about for a sense of closure, he said decisively, "Now let us turn to page 294 as we continue with our service."

Joseph turned back from the bima, ambling slowly toward his chair perched on the side wall between the ark and Vivian, who nodded with approval. He cupped and combed his gray beard with his fingers, wondering whether he truly believed what he said. After many years of turning and turning and turning over sacred texts, it was harder to think new thoughts and spin them into clear proclamations. When he was not recycling old sermons, which he calculated he could do after seven years of letting them lay fallow in his files, he often grasped onto new ideas that popped into his head without letting them solidify, or that others had stated in his presence that he could enrich with his own commentary. His polished delivery could frequently disguise his doubt.

Joseph viewed himself, and the general role of rabbi, as a scholar first. As a seminary student in the 1970s, he had pored over the Talmud's puzzles with deep anticipation, as if they were prayers themselves, as if, somehow, speaking them aloud could bring sense to the chaos all around. His dedicated study even spawned a subtle hunch, preventing Joseph from standing fully upright, a malady in which he took a strange pride.

As Joseph grew in his profession in the following decade,

however, he found that his congregants were not concerned with situating their religious choices in an age-old tradition. Rather, they came to his synagogue to hear a voice that sounded like their own—though a bit wiser—that confirmed their choices. What mattered was the sermon, not study. So, Joseph trained himself to be a better speaker, to choose shorter, digestible texts to share that his congregants would accept and would contemplate. At least for the duration of a two-hour service.

Sammy Bickel, a fixture at Beth Abraham for decades, took Joseph's place at the bima to begin leading the congregation in prayer. Since the cantor passed away two years before, and the board decided not to rehire for the role, the few members literate in prayer-leading were called upon more and more to do so. As Sammy, sporting one of his signature bowties, carried the Torah around the sanctuary in order to return it to the ark, Joseph continued to mull over his most recent words.

Is it really true? he wondered. That we need to, or even can, create more space for the younger Jews, the entitled ones who seem to want meaning in every moment, but are not willing to dedicate the necessary effort? The children of my congregants, who still act like needy, misbehaved children from Sunday school? My own children and grandchildren who seem to believe this tradition is an uncomfortable coat they put on a few times a year?

Suddenly, a loud thump jolted Joseph from his thoughts. He looked around the room. Sammy Bickel was on the ground, stuck in an uncomfortable prostration in front of the ark. Underneath him was the fallen scroll. The congregation let out a loud, collective gasp.

Sammy Bickel had dropped the Torah.

It was Vivian who reached him first. As Joseph rose from his seat, he hesitated. Should he first tend to Sammy Bickel, his long-time congregant, a friend, he might even say? Or was his responsibility to the Torah, the most sacred and fragile object of the Jewish tradition?

Frozen in his dilemma, he watched as Vivian put a hand on Sammy's lower back and knelt down to the floor, to his eye level, her short, brown curls covering her mouth. Even so, Joseph could tell that she was whispering consoling words with no hesitation. Though she was still quite new to the role, he thought, it was as if she were trained for this precise moment.

Joseph strode over to retrieve the Torah, sticking out from underneath Sammy. He noticed that the top of one of the wooden spindles was chipped. He picked up the Torah gently, not wanting to harm it any more, wanting to channel deep love toward its wounds. He hugged it tightly, closing his eyes and wishing it healing. He carefully returned it to the open ark.

As he turned back toward Sammy, who was now surrounded by a crowd of congregants, tears sprung from Joseph's eyes. He felt a rupture, as though the pain absorbed by the Torah was now his pain. Joseph could see Vivian through the cracks in the crowd of bodies, soliciting the assistance of others to help raise Sammy from the floor.

When Sammy stood, he was weeping. There was a damp circle on the red carpet where his face had been. Sammy repeated over and over, "How could this be? How could this be?" He took a few inelegant steps toward the ark and kissed the Torah.

The commotion continued as congregants comforted

Sammy and wondered aloud what would happen now. Some knew that dropping the Torah was a grievous matter, while others intuited as much.

After letting a few minutes pass, after Sammy had been guided toward one of the plush chairs and everyone else returned to their seats, Joseph lightly shushed the crowd. He racked his mind for the right words. "My friends," he began, "a Torah is one of our most prized possessions, and so is the welfare of our fellow congregants. Let us continue our service and direct our prayers to the healing of our beloved Torah, and our beloved Sammy. We will later consider how to respond as a congregation. But for now, let us pray."

Joseph stepped in to take Sammy's place leading the service. But as he stood there, in front of the whole congregation, the words would not come. He could only stare, feeling a deep pain as he pictured the chipped spindle that now rested behind the closed doors of the ark.

In the midst of this daze, Joseph felt a palm on his shoulder and heard a whisper in his ear. "Would you prefer if I continued the service?" Vivian said. Joseph nodded, walked back to his seat on the bima, and sat down, not blinking, just staring ahead.

Joseph had been present once before when a Torah was dropped. It was decades ago, when he was a teenager in Boston. The drop had come at a vulnerable time. Synagogue membership had been slowly dwindling, with many moving from the city center out to the suburbs. When the Torah fell to the floor, it felt like a divine message that it was time for the congregation to move or close its doors. It would not survive in its original location.

Vivian began to sing a niggun, choosing a slow, minor melody reserved for the service of communal repentance on Yom Kippur. She sang it once through alone as the congregation listened to her soothing voice. When the tune started a second time, a few joined in, and when the third round began, most of the congregants sang together. They continued for a few minutes before returning to the regularly scheduled prayer. When they did, it was time for the Amidah, an opportunity for each congregant's silent meditation. In her own prayer, Vivian modeled a humble pose, hunching her back and furrowing her eyebrows.

Some congregants mirrored her stance while others fidgeted uncomfortably. Discomfort settled in the space of the silence. Throughout the few minutes of quiet, Sammy Bickel interrupted with echoing grunts. He was still crying.

After the Amidah, Vivian continued the service as usual, though an uneasiness lingered in the sanctuary. Something was off. When the service ended, president Harry Mermelstein, a tall, sturdy man whose full head of brown hair was graying at the roots, who moved through the world with an unquestioned confidence, gave the announcements as if nothing out of the ordinary had happened. But of course, what had happened was anything but ordinary.

TWO

MEMBERS OF THE congregation cleared out of the sanctuary, leaving more quickly than usual, as if to shake off the events of the day. Vivian and Joseph made immediate plans to stay and discuss what had happened. They jogged over to a few key leaders to request their attendance. In addition to Harry Mermelstein, they tapped Vera Cohen, the vice president (and with her husband, Charlie, a significant donor to Beth Abraham), and Tamar Benayoun, the head of the ritual committee.

The group gathered in Joseph's office. They were seated around a long, mahogany table, surrounded by books and sports jerseys featuring the names of New England teams in Hebrew lettering.

"That was quite a service," Joseph began.

"It sure was! I've only ever heard stories about a Torah falling, from when my dad was a kid in Tunis," Tamar said. "It was considered a bad sign for the community."

"We aren't superstitious like that anymore. Are we? Rabbi?" Harry said.

Vivian knew that Harry was always referring to Joseph when he asked questions ending in "Rabbi."

Joseph took his cue. "Well, Harry, dropping a Torah is a serious matter. The rabbis required the man—I mean," he stuttered, "the, uh, person—who dropped the Torah to fast for forty days as an act of repentance. But given that this is an unrealistic demand to place on Sammy Bickel, there is an alternative option that all who witnessed the event share the fast. So, we could ask everyone who was at today's service to sign up for individual days of our communal fast."

"That seems like a lot to ask," Tamar said. "We don't really believe that something bad would happen otherwise, do we? I mean…." She stared out the window behind Joseph. "I know that antisemitism is on the rise…but that couldn't be…." She left her thought unresolved.

"We all felt it," Vera spoke up, "when the Torah dropped. The, the, the off-ness. And Tamar's right. It is a scary time. I think people want to feel safe and empowered in our community. Perhaps this fast can do the job."

"The rabbis also consider tzedakah to be an appropriate response to dropping a Torah," Vivian said, building off of what Vera proposed. "Perhaps we could use this as an opportunity to collect money, or better yet, participate in some volunteering in

the city. We need a ritual or some kind of action that is going to
be a *tikkun*, a repair."

"We could do both!" Vera said with enthusiasm.

"That just doesn't seem efficient," Harry said. "Getting
forty people to fast is already a logistical nightmare. If we have
to do it, we have to do it. It's the law. But let's not make too
much work for everyone."

Vera and Harry sat comfortably on opposing sides of most
synagogue business. Vera represented what Harry called the
"touchy-feely" faction of the community—the ones who had
their own meditation minyan, the ones who encouraged service leaders to sing new tunes, and sometimes, the ones who
pushed the community to take stands Harry did not think
appropriate.

"Whether or not it's the law is debatable," Vivian said, sitting up straighter. "It's an interpretation of law, like most of our
practices and rituals. It's a reflection of the general significance
we place on the Torah and the sacredness it holds for us. The
ritual surrounding it is based on a feeling that when a Torah
drops, it may be symbolic of some sort of rupture. And so, we
create a symbolic antidote."

Joseph shifted in his seat. "Now, let's not get confused
between tradition, law and lore. We can choose to read whatever we want into the Torah dropping. The fact of the matter
is, a beloved member of our community slipped. There was no
ill intent, and we were able to help Sammy get back to his feet,
gently return the Torah and carry on with the service.

"I propose," Joseph continued, "that I write a letter to the
community stating just that and soliciting the congregation for

forty volunteers to fast one day each. I will even sign up for the first day. And that will be that."

"Whatever you say, Rabbi," Tamar said. She had only recently been elected to the board, to lead the ritual committee in preparing for holidays and ensuring that Shabbat services ran smoothly. She was not too inclined to step out of line.

"Fine." Harry grumbled in half-hearted support. He was starting to rise from his seat at the head of the table, when Vera spoke up.

"I don't want to drop the idea of giving tzedakah or volunteering. Some congregants have discussed a desire to get more involved in the broader Providence community and this could be a great opportunity to show our commitment outside the walls of our synagogue."

A subtle smile appeared on Vivian's face, despite her best attempt to hide it. Joseph furrowed his brow.

"Tell you what, Vera," Harry said, folding his hands and placing his two pointer fingers over his mouth, as if they were in a business negotiation. "Why don't you take this to the social justice committee, ask them to make a recommendation of how we might respond to this, um, incident, and then bring it back to the board?"

"That could work," Vera said, elongating her words. "But our next meeting isn't for another two weeks." After retiring from a local homelessness-advocacy nonprofit several years earlier, Vera had thrown herself deeply into synagogue leadership, now sitting on three different committees. She considered her next move. "Maybe a subcommittee can meet about it before then."

"It's settled then," Harry said. "After Shabbat, Rabbi Glass will write a letter to the congregation detailing today's events and inviting members to fast for one of the next forty days. And Vera and the social justice team will work on a response through charity or community service or something."

Joseph exhaled with relief. "Yes. It's settled. Thank you for summarizing, Harry."

As Vivian locked the doors to the building a few minutes later, she felt a familiar frustration. This was how Harry always seemed to deal with challenges: by delegating them to a committee where, most often, they would disappear.

THREE

VIVIAN, ALONG WITH the Reverend Lisa Carpenter, of the Unitarian Universalist congregation down the street from Beth Abraham, and the Reverend Heather Wu, from an Episcopal church across town, was guided by a hostess to a back booth at the Hideaway Café, where they often brunched when their days off aligned. There, they would regale each other with tales from life and work over mimosas and stacks of blueberry pancakes.

The Hideaway, which sat on the line between the city and the suburbs, had opened among a wave of coffee shops and hip brunch spots that popped up all over the north side of Providence. The walls were red, the floors checkered, and, for some reason, there were life-sized, bronzed dogs perched throughout the cafe.

Settling into their regular spot, guarded by a Great Dane with a troubling stare, each woman did one last check for nearby congregants—a move Heather had dubbed "the swivel." Lisa let out a luxurious groan. The coast was clear.

"Everyone in the congregation keeps asking to touch my baby bump!" Heather said, jumping right in. "Some don't *even* ask. How can people think that's okay? Like, I'm their pastor, so they get to know everything about me? They get to touch me? God, what's it going to be like when the baby is born?" She sipped her water. "Last week I preached about Jesus multiplying the fish and bread loaves, and the importance of recognizing our own abundance and what that demands of us. And the first thing I heard after the service was, 'Looks like you're about to do some multiplying of your own.' That is not okay!"

"Wow. I'm so sorry to hear that. How did that make you feel?" Lisa said.

"Oh, Lisa, don't pastor me. Clearly it made me feel pretty fucking angry."

"Sorry. Sometimes it's hard to turn that off," Lisa said. "Maybe you could put a sign on your belly that says 'Off limits?'"

"Have you talked to Bill about it?" Vivian asked.

Heather sighed. "He's not really an ally. He's still adjusting to the idea of me going on maternity leave, and whenever I bring it up, he gets so stressed. I've learned to pick my battles with him. He says and believes that he's supportive, but it's like he thinks he's doing me a favor by not being a total asshole." Heather sighed.

The waitress approached their table to take their orders. Blueberry pancakes for Vivian and Heather, and a western omelet for Lisa. Vivian rubbed her hands together as she ordered, eager to eat her first post-Passover pancakes.

After the waitress left, Heather continued. "It's a culture problem in our church, and if Bill doesn't play a role in naming it, as the senior minister, I don't think it's going to shift. Because I've already negotiated the maternity leave I wanted, I don't want to ask for anything more."

"Sounds more like you've made the calculation not to ask for anything more," Vivian said.

"It's so hard to win," Lisa jumped in.

"Heck, we don't need a full win, or even a touchdown. I'd take a field goal. Or just a safety," Vivian said.

"You and your perplexing sports references," Heather groaned. "You know we have no clue what you just said, right?"

"You really should learn. It's the best way to connect with older male congregants," Vivian said, sipping her water. "I'm telling you: life-changing!"

Vivian had met Heather at some clergy meeting or other soon after she started her job. It was hard to keep track of what important encounters happened at which unimportant meetings. After noticing a few instances of synchronized eye-rolling at something offensive but unmemorable, Vivian had introduced herself. And then Heather introduced Vivian to Lisa.

Pointing to Vivian's folded-up newspaper at the edge of the table, Lisa changed the subject. "Are either of you thinking much about the special election for Mayor?"

The *Providence Chronicle* had run profiles of the three

Democratic candidates competing to fill the seat of former mayor Al DeSoto, who had died in January of a sudden heart attack. First there was Mike McCann, city councilor for a ward in the northeast section of the city. He had won his seat by only two percentage points in a low-turnout election. But when DeSoto died, McCann had been appointed mayor pro tempore for three months, per city guidelines. During that time, the unions cozied up to him and he ingratiated himself to some influential players by signing off on a few big development deals.

Then there was Margaret Heath, a civil rights lawyer who had won some high-profile housing discrimination cases tried in Rhode Island's Supreme Court and whose policy proposals sat to the left of McCann's. Lastly, there was Alex Santiago, a young unknown leader coming out of activist circles whom not many were taking seriously.

As they dug into their brunch, Vivian summarized the article for Lisa and Heather, offering her own editorial. McCann was the lackluster frontrunner as a result of active union support and strong financial backing. Heath was positioning herself as the right choice for pragmatic progressives. And though no one was giving him much of a chance, Alex Santiago would maybe move the others more to the left.

"I saw Santiago speak a few times at protests calling out police violence against Black lives, and he was compelling," Lisa said, chomping on a mouthful of omelet. "But Bree has worked with Heath on some affordable housing projects and thinks she'd make a great mayor." Bree Parker, Lisa's partner, sometimes joined the brunches when she could sneak away from her

office at the South Side Community Development Corpora-
tion. "I guess we'll get the chance to see all of them for ourselves at the Interfaith Council's forum."

"I find the routine of that event to be uninspiring," Heather
said, wiping syrup off her chin. "The candidates don't care
much about what we have to say. They just make boilerplate
statements of what they think we want to hear."

"Well, they do care about what *some* of us have to say," Vivian said.

"Yeah?" Lisa said, settling comfortably into her seat, recognizing from the look in Vivian's eyes that she would be listening
for a while.

Vivian moved in closer, planting her elbows on the table.
"Big donors," she said. "But, more importantly, developers.
They run this city. And some of them are our congregants.
When I was in rabbinical school in New York, there was a big
kerfuffle over the city possibly hosting the Olympics. I had a
crush on this community organizer who was really involved, so
I decided to join the fight too."

"Ooh, what happened with her?" Lisa interjected.

Vivian paid no attention to the question. "You know who
wants a city to host the Olympics? Developers and the hotel
industry and that's about it. One of the key boosters was a huge
donor at the synagogue where I interned. I'd secretly go to ral-
lies against this guy, but he was in my congregation."

"Hmm. I always thought the Olympics were awesome. But,
as per usual, go ahead and yuck my yum," Heather said, putting
her feet up on the otherwise unoccupied booth.

"At least now you'll know how I became so insufferable,"

Vivian joked. "There was a lot of pressure on the city to pull the bid to host, once residents realized they were getting a bad deal and would have to cover any cost overruns with their own tax money. The developers didn't come out looking too good, since very few of the projects they proposed would have benefitted city residents. The guy leading the charge, the one from my synagogue, took a real beating in the papers, but he was still the golden boy of the congregation after he made a big donation to save face. And I bet that wasn't his only big donation."

Lisa snuck her fork over and stole half a pancake from Vivian's barely touched plate. Unfazed, Vivian continued her diatribe. "These guys order what's on the menu before any of us get into the restaurant. They make their millions in backroom deals, spend some of it on P.R. to spin a good story, and the rest of us don't know what hit us." Vivian gulped her mimosa, resting her case.

"Barry Brook, who runs CK Construction—he's on our board at St. James," Heather said, leaning in and folding her arms, betraying her former posture of disinterest. "Always sponsors the church's Easter celebration and gave the most seed money for the capital campaign a few years ago. A real *macher*, you might say."

"He must have cashed in on that influence at some point," Vivian said. "We've got one too. Will Gould, the CEO of Riverside Developers." She took another sip and continued. "When I was growing up, the stories of unbounded authority were all about rabbis. My cousins are Orthodox, and when their rabbi said jump, they all jumped. They needed his advice and approval for everything.

"One time, for Passover, they asked him what to feed their beloved goldfish, Gragger, because the fish food didn't have proper kosher certification. He told them to feed it matza meal. Matza meal! Which expands enough within human digestive systems to make us all constipated for eight days."

"So, not a great call for a fish?" Lisa asked.

"By the fourth day, the fish was triple its size and it exploded and died."

"That's so sad," Lisa said.

"It's infuriating, is what it is. And my cousins, my aunt, my uncle, just didn't get it. Their rabbi killed the fish with an unfounded and dangerous ruling!"

Heather took another big bite of pancakes. "So, I guess that's the origin story for your skepticism of authority?"

"You could say that." Another rabbi came to Vivian's mind, her childhood rabbi, who had half of Cincinnati wrapped around his finger: the Conservative Jews, the other rabbis in town, the politicians. And she thought of her mom who, along with several other women, walked out of a Shabbat service in public protest after learning that he had had affairs with female congregants for years, and none of those who had known, not the board nor other congregants, had done a thing about it.

"In the Orthodox world, people would follow their rabbi without question. But here, the whole power structure has been turned on its head. Rabbis or not, we are just more pawns beholden to the rich guys, like everyone else."

"Come on, that's harsh," Lisa said. "There's more to it. Yesterday, we welcomed a newborn into our community. The parents had been trying for years and had given up, and then finally it happened. And the community surrounded them with so much support. People crave connection, support, celebration, and we—"

"Man, can't we ever just talk about what normal women talk about?" Heather asked. "I'm moving on. Viv, have you gone on any good dates lately?"

Vivian cut a slice of pancake and chewed slowly.

"Are you ever going to get back to me about my friend Liz?" Lisa said, filling in the space Vivian was not. "Come on. She's funny. She's a PhD student in biology. Good dancer. And she's pretty hot. Just go for it."

"Thanks, Lisa. We've gone over this. She sounds great, but people don't get it when I tell them I'm a rabbi. They don't think I'm a normal person. How did Liz take it when you broke the news?"

"I said she's a rabbi, but she's awesome."

"*But*? You're a freaking minister and even you have to make disclaimers for me?"

"Maybe you should just date other queer rabbis?" Heather said.

"Been there, done that, and it's not happening again," Vivian said. "Story for another time."

"So, what's your plan?" Lisa asked.

"I don't know. I go on Jewish meditation retreats. I'm hoping that yields some success."

Heather slammed her fork down on the table. "That's not a plan!"

"Trust me, Jewish meditation retreats—heck, regular meditation retreats—are bursting at the seams with queer, Jewish women, or at least Jewish women who could be queer under the right conditions."

"Why not just go on one date with my friend?" Lisa implored.

"I'll think about it." Vivian shifted gears. "But let's just close the loop on the mayor's race."

"Smooth pivot," Lisa said.

"This city is gentrifying so rapidly, and we're all a part of that. What if we made it clear that we, our faith communities, cared about things like building more affordable housing?"

"It sounds like you're gearing up to run," Lisa joked.

"I'm with you, Viv. We say we care about immigrants, but we aren't doing much while families are being separated and kids are getting caged," Heather said. "We couldn't even promote or go to a rally as a congregation a few years back, because it was 'too political.'"

"Hmm, I wonder who was behind that," Vivian said.

Heather scowled. "Barry Brook."

Vivian chuckled, raising her empty mimosa glass. "And our senior clergy and out-of-touch board presidents wonder why young people don't come to our congregations."

FOUR

Harry Mermelstein was stressed. Sitting in the mustard-yellow Beth Abraham office, he shuffled through the membership files. 307 member units. Some families had joined in recent years, but more were leaving, or dying. When Harry and his family joined, more than two decades back, the congregation had already been nowhere near its peak numbers. Religion was a tough business, he thought, each time Joseph confided his concern about keeping the doors open (and by extension, the survival of the Jewish people).

As the retired CEO of Goodies, a small high-end supermarket chain, Harry knew how to run an operation: bookkeeping, staff oversight, building maintenance. These tasks fell under the purview of Cindy Carlson, Beth Abraham's executive director, but Cindy had fallen ill with pneumonia and was taking a while to recover. In the meantime, Harry decided, as president of the board, to throw himself into the logistical business of the synagogue until Cindy returned.

Harry calculated that amiably stepping in to cover for Cindy would additionally earn him points with the factions of congregants that had not warmed to his presidency. Some, including Vera, were suspicious of Harry's systems: budget cuts, timesheet tracking, staff reviews. She would say as much at board meetings. But Harry was proud of the progress he was making to get things in order. "Turning another business around," he would say to his friends.

The front doorbell rang, and Harry jumped up from his desk and marched down the hall to answer.

"Hey, Bob, let's make this quick," Harry said, greeting the city inspector in the doorway. "I know we've both got places to be and things to do."

"Hiya, Harry," said the inspector, Bob Stills, as he rummaged through his briefcase and pulled out a clipboard. Bob, an old acquaintance of Harry's, was a plump bureaucrat who stood with a tired slump. He waved his arm, motioning Harry to step outside.

Bob began walking slowly around the building's exterior, as Harry trailed behind. Looking up, Bob jumped right to business. "I see that you did your due diligence on these branches," referring to a tree whose limbs used to creep toward the electrical wires.

He climbed through the budding rose bushes, avoiding

thorn pricks, and studied each window's caulking. "Seems like the place is well insulated," Bob said, "but you might want to upgrade your windows in the next few years. There are better models coming out all the time. And the city is on this going-green kick, so it's part of the gig now to make recommendations about saving energy." Bob turned his attention to the roof. "Are you thinking about getting solar panels? If you take the plunge, you get a discount from the city and an ad in your honor in the *Chronicle* saying you signed onto our 'I Green Providence' campaign."

"We did some preliminary research a while back," Harry said, "and it's just too much money up front. To get us to shell out for that, you'd have to sweeten the deal. I mean, come on, 5% and a picture in the paper?"

"You'd be surprised at how many people think that's a worthwhile incentive, Harry."

"Those people must not be very good businessmen."

"All right, all right, let's keep it moving," Bob said. "I want to check the pipes. This winter did a number on a lot of the copper plumbing systems around town." They continued to trace the building's exterior. Bob entered through an unmarked door into the boiler room, where he inspected the furnace and the dusty jungle of metal crisscrossing the ceiling.

"These seem fine," Bob said, checking off more boxes on his clipboard. "But if you have any issues with the heat or water supply, make sure to get a plumber in quickly. There've been a bunch of burst pipes these past few months." He continued on into a hallway. Harry followed, thumbing through emails on his phone.

Bob checked the smoke alarm, the carbon monoxide detectors, the heating system. "Looking good, Harry," Bob said, experimenting with the vent pressure in the main hallway. "Say, I heard on the news that some synagogues around the country have been getting bomb threats. And then there was that shooting last year. How are things here?"

"We're definitely rattled," Harry said, looking up from his phone. "Especially some of the older congregants, who, you know, think about, well...." Harry's eyes got big, as if he was asking Bob to fill in the blank. "We're in talks with the police chief about increasing security. He's been sending officers to do loops around the building, monitor our more well-attended services. Chief Thicke has always been a good friend to us."

"Sounds like you've got the right people on your team. And I'll bet, if McCann is our next mayor, he'll be a good guy to have on your side too." Bob caught himself. "Saying that as a private citizen, off the record, of course."

"Mike's promising. He's got strong endorsements," Harry said. "Will Gould told me that he's hosting a fundraiser for Mike in a few weeks."

Bob looked up from his clipboard. "Are you friends with Gould?"

"Yes siree. And he's been very good to the synagogue."

"In this city, with a guy like Gould on your side, I wouldn't think you even need to go through the bureaucratic motions of an inspection," Bob joked.

"I like to follow the rules, Bob," Harry said. "It keeps things predictable, and people can't expose you if cashing in your favors backfires."

After Bob checked the lead levels in the Hebrew school classrooms and the patching of old leaks in the sanctuary, they made their way down the hall to the kitchen. Raymond Weeks, Beth Abraham's custodian and handyman, was kneeling down taking measurements of the stove.

"My man, Raymond!" Harry greeted him. Raymond turned toward the two men entering. "Raymond, this is Bob Stills, the city inspector. He's just making sure that everything is up to code. Bob, this is Raymond, the guy who really runs the place."

"Morning, Bob," Raymond said with a forced smile, and turned back to his task.

Bob asked Raymond what he was up to.

"We're getting ready to upgrade some appliances in here," Harry said, before Raymond could speak. "It's been a long time coming. The burners have been finicky, and we could use a bigger oven."

Raymond continued to work in silence. Bob moved around the kitchen turning various switches on and off.

"So, uh, it's looking like the Sox are gearing up for another run into October," Harry started, remembering a story or two Raymond had shared from baseball seasons past. "Raymond, you and the missus going to make it to Boston for any games this season?"

"We're more of a Pawtucket Sox family," Raymond said. "Our nephew made it onto the team a few years ago. He couldn't hack it in the end, but we still like going in the summertime."

Harry and Raymond had moved through the same space for almost two decades without exchanging much more than pleasantries. As president of the synagogue, Harry felt he ought to get to know the staff better, but moving past routine greetings was taking time. Knowing nothing about minor league baseball, Harry nodded and walked over to the corner where Bob was examining the refrigerator wiring. The two men soon marched out of the kitchen toward the front entrance, leaving Raymond to his task.

As Bob followed Harry back outside the building, he looked to his left at an empty expanse. "Harry, are you all ever going to do anything with that piece of land?"

"Past boards have had ideas of expanding, or of building an assisted living community here," Harry said. "But you know how bureaucracy works, eh, Bob? And you compound that with the habits of a bunch of Jews, coming to a decision is pretty hopeless." They took a few more steps toward the parking lot, both looking toward the empty plot.

Bob shaped his fingers like an L and put them up to his eye as if he was looking through a camera, or taking measurements. "Must be pretty valuable in this market."

"Oh, it is. Now that I'm in charge, selling it off is a priority. We'll be looking for offers and I think we'll make a move soon."

Bob paused as he checked off the last set of boxes on his clipboard. "All right, Harry. Everything looks fine here. You'll be getting your updated inspection certification soon." He walked with purpose toward his grey Ford sedan.

"You Jews run a tight ship," Bob shouted back, as he opened his trunk. "Even if you are a bunch of cheapskates."

Harry laughed as he shut the front door.

FIVE

"**P**ASS THE WHISKEY," Will Gould said.

"All right, Will, but don't give me any crap about the brand," Fred responded.

On the top floor of the tallest building in Providence, overlooking the point where the Providence River is fed by the Seekonk, sat four of the most powerful people in the city: Barry Brook, Will Gould, Mark Scaccia, and Mark Frederick (whom they called Fred, so as not to mix him up with Scaccia). They were gathered for a one p.m. lunch meeting, reclining in the buttery leather chairs and surrounded by the mahogany-paneled walls of Radclyffe's Lounge, on the twenty-sixth floor.

"When have I ever given you crap about the brand?" Will said.

Fred groaned. "You kidding me? At the last meeting. Some of us just have to run a tighter whiskey budget. Okay?"

"Whiskey is whiskey is whiskey, isn't it?" Mark chimed in.

"Make a few more mil a year, Mark. Then we'll talk," Barry joked, as he tore into a prime rib, holding his fork at a distance to avoid staining his silk tie.

"How's Julie, Will?" Mark asked.

"Oh, you know how it is," Will said. "She's been eyeing a few pieces from some up-and-coming Italian artist. So she's in Sicily, making offers, spending my money. You know how they are when they get their hearts set on something."

"You don't need to tell me twice," Barry said. "Mary's chairing the hospital gala and has been yapping in my ear about it for weeks. I can't wait until it's over."

"I keep telling you guys. Just move on to the second wife. Go younger and less ambitious, and you won't have to deal with these pet projects." Fred could always be relied upon to push the envelope a bit.

"All right, gentlemen, let's get to business," Barry began. "I hear from city hall that the property tax hike is back on the table. Last time this came up, it was pretty easy to squash, but not in boom time. The schools, the parks, and all the agencies want it to go through so they can claim some of the windfall."

"This shouldn't be too hard. We just make a case for the old tax breaks, right?" Mark asked, examining a big chunk of meat on his fork.

"Well, there's been a lot of scrutiny of tax breaks ever since the *Chronicle*'s exposé about the Ridgetown project. The city is going to be cautious this time around," Barry said.

"Let's just throw more ad revenue at the *Chronicle*, maybe some of the TV stations," Will said. "They're struggling these days. They'd do anything for some cash. It'll buy us a few years, enough to flip all the land that's worth developing in this city anyway."

Though the four real estate developers sometimes competed for contracts, each man had his area of expertise. Barry was the commercial guy, Will the high-end condo guy, Mark the mid-range condo guy, and Fred the speculation guy. Sometimes they dabbled in one another's realms, but during the development boom, there were plenty of jobs to go around.

They met every few months to ensure they could attack whatever obstacles came their way. There was enough shared interest to make the fragile alliance beneficial for all. And any excuse to consume expensed steak and whiskey was a win in their books.

"It's trickier this time around, but we've got the head start we need," Barry said, wiping steak sauce from his mouth with a napkin.

"That's right! The tax hike may not even be on the liberals' radar, what with all the ridiculous identity politicking that consumes their time," Fred said.

"Let's see…let's see," Will continued. "I'll bet we can get the average renter on our side. If we can push some stories out there about landlords being forced to raise rents, we could skew the initial polls and steer clear of a ballot question."

"No matter what, we stick to our bread and butter," Barry said. "Jobs. Jobs. Jobs. We call on the unions. We pull out our glossy reports and reiterate who's employing the people of Providence."

"One fly in the ointment is the mayor's race," Will added. "DeSoto was good to us, and we were good to him."

"It's a shame he croaked," Fred laughed, gulping down some more whiskey. "He knew how to stay out of the way."

Will stared at Fred. He didn't disagree with the sentiment, but he never would reach Fred's level of disregard for social propriety. "*DeSoto*'s housing team is still calling the shots over there," Will said, moving on. "But we've got to maintain our grip. McCann's obviously our guy."

"So, let's send lots of money his way," Barry suggested. "He proved himself when he was interim mayor. Any value in testing the waters with Alex Santiago, to see what leverage there might be with him? Those radical types can change their tune when money starts rolling in."

Will shook his head. "Sometimes that works, but not with him. He's too strident. And he's got no chance of winning."

"And Margaret Heath?" Mark asked.

"No!" Fred yelped. "That firebrand wouldn't accept it anyway. She keeps trying to sue us to build more housing for freeloaders. No! We take her down with campaign ads."

"It's not just her. Santiago's base will definitely bring up the tax breaks and gentrification and yada, yada, yada during the election," Barry said. "So let's pull out all the stops when it's called for."

Fred sipped his whiskey. "Even before it's called for! We are important men, with important work to do. We've got to stay ahead of the game."

They all continued gnawing on their steaks. Will shifted gears. "Mark, at some point, a property on Banks Street is going on the market. Perfect for condos. I'd appreciate if you wouldn't bid on it. My synagogue is selling it; they've been holding it for a while with big plans. But surprise, surprise, they never sealed the deal."

"Ha, it must be all those goddamn board meetings. All that democracy—it just means nothing ever gets done." Fred said.

"What's your plan?" Mark asked.

"I'm going to cut them a deal by leveraging a loan from the city," Will said. "I've thrown a lot of money their way over the past decade, so I don't foresee much trouble."

The men stood to return to their offices for their two o'clocks. Fred circled his plate with his finger, retrieving the remaining steak sauce and licking it off. "That's right. Always ahead of the game!"

SIX

VIVIAN EXAMINED THE cars on Corbett Road. Two Lexuses. A Mercedes. And some fancy SUVs. She felt self-conscious about the dented bumper on her decade-old Honda Accord. Corbett was one of those Providence streets that looked like it belonged in an expensive suburb rather than within city limits.

Vivian vacillated between righteous judgment and feelings of inadequacy when in close proximity to the wealth of her congregants. Currently, she was parked outside of Farah Rice's six-bedroom colonial, the house immaculately framed by evergreen shrubs. She hesitated to call and let Farah know she had arrived. The scale tipped toward inadequacy.

They would soon be heading across town together to the Providence Interfaith Council's mayoral candidate forum, hosted by Heather's church. Vivian had done what she could to recruit members of her congregation to attend. The previous week, she had arrived at the meeting of the social justice committee with a plan.

The committee's work up to now had primarily entailed doling out donations to the local food pantry and persuading the congregation to put a rainbow flag on its website. Regarding the matter of the rainbow flag, victory had come after a tense and drawn-out board process of nearly a year. The advocates had surveyed Beth Abraham membership, written two supportive articles in the congregational bulletin, and sought out Joseph for monthly meetings to encourage his involvement. The opposition—a few conservative members who felt this to be too public a declaration—held out for a while. But they grew frustrated attending all the necessary meetings, and finally, they had relented. The victors, of whom Farah Rice was one, had sponsored a kiddush in honor of the feat. A spread of hot kugels was ordered for the occasion, a luxury which was usually only merited by bar and bat mitzvahs.

The most recent committee meeting began with a long conversation about what tzedakah project the group wanted to propose as a response to the Torah drop a few weeks before. Vera suggested they use the opportunity to forge new connections with a local organization working to resettle refugee families. But most agreed that it would be easier to encourage members to take on a shift at the food pantry or bring some extra donated cans.

Vivian had learned to put on an interested face for these meetings. Joseph used to regularly attend, but when she was hired, he easily parted ways with that responsibility and added it to her job description. She looked for opportunities to nudge the members in small ways, and the Interfaith Council forum offered an opening. She made a light pitch for attending the event together. But the date coincided with opera commitments and a lecture by a renowned Bangladeshi author visiting Brown University.

Finally, a few women agreed to attend if someone else would drive them. Vivian offered to take two of them: Farah and Sally Schwartz-Kaplan, both in their seventies, and both stalwart Beth Abraham members who had served on too many congregational committees to count. In total, Vivian left the meeting with six yeses. She had learned to temper her expectations about work, and about most things: romantic relationships, her beloved Cincinnati Bengals. She would take all the field goals she could get.

Even though St. James Episcopal Church was only a short distance away, before the trip, Vivian agonized over what the women would discuss in the car. She was wary of getting too personal. She was familiar with the challenges of both women's personal lives: for instance, that Sally and Herb were considering divorce after years of squabbling and therapy. But Vivian did not want to act too formal, either, and she desperately wanted to avoid the incessant national news cycle that she knew, from past experience, would send Farah down a spiral of despair.

So, Vivian had thought up conversational topics prior to the car ride. New Year's resolutions, Elena Ferrante novels, condo construction along the main roads. And if that did not work, she knew that the classic rock station was on a Beatles-only kick for the week.

After Farah settled into the car, Vivian drove the two blocks to Sally's, and they were on their way. Vivian was relieved when Sally initiated a conversation about a movie she had seen with her "girlfriend" over the weekend. (When Vivian's congregants used that term, it always made her chuckle and imagine an alternate Beth Abraham full of lesbian entanglements among the older women.)

The movie Sally had seen was a romantic comedy with that British actor who always played the same character. But just as the conversation gained momentum, Sally abruptly stopped sharing her summary of the plot. "Oh, I guess we shouldn't discuss the movie I saw on Shabbat with the Rabbi in the car. Uh, so, ladies, what's new with you?"

No one spoke. Vivian was looking to the landmarks outside the car for inspiration, but there was none to be found. She remembered her list of conversational topics. "Did you know that the first of Nisan, the month we are in now, is one of four 'new years' in our calendar? We get so many chances to reflect. What are your hopes for this new year?"

"I guess not to see so many movies on Shabbat," Sally said. The silence continued. Vivian opted for the Beatles marathon. A few minutes later, they arrived at St. James, which, for a buiding Vivian passed several times a week, was looking unexpectedly foreign today, with its large cross sitting atop the looming steeple.

"Wow, that is quite a cross," Sally said in a higher pitch than usual. Vivian was familiar with this discomfort. When she was younger, she would often ask to visit the church around the corner from her house. She loved the music of the bells that marked time. She wanted to see them, perhaps even ring them. But Vivian's mother, Sharon, would clench Vivian's hand a little tighter as they walked past, anticipating that request. For Vivian, the consistency of this pattern—at six years old, then seven, then eight—made it clear that she should stop asking.

"All right, ladies," she said. "Let's go in."

SEVEN

S T. JAMES'S SANCTUARY was all peach walls and partitioned, cherrywood pews. Vivian wondered how a community could maintain its bonds while obstructed by these barriers. Looking toward the front of the room, she saw Heather caught up in an important-seeming conversation near the sound system. This was not the Hideaway Café. Vivian decided to wait and greet her friend after the program.

Examining the room more thoroughly, Vivian spotted the rest of the Beth Abraham delegation in a middle pew. She was satisfied by her modest victory, wrangling a handful of congregants to engage in this local political ritual. She wondered if there were seeds of something new here.

The local politicans knew Joseph. As a key representative of Jewish Providence, it was he who was invited each year to give the invocation at the city's MLK Day breakfast. It seemed to Vivian that Joseph understood that playing the game served the synagogue well.

She knew the story. She could repeat it, and sometimes found herself doing just that when the situation called for it. Joseph had arrived at a congregation in transition in the early '80s. While Jews had been in Providence since the turn of the century, over the decades prior to Joseph's installation, more Jews in the city had acquired their own businesses, gained influence in real estate, and become active players in local politics.

Several weeks into his tenure, Joseph had arrived at work and noticed some graffiti on the side of the building. "Go home," it read, in large block lettering. "Home?" Vivian could hear Joseph say as she repeated the story in her head. She imagined him staring at the words for minutes without blinking.

"What other home did they have? Poland? The country my father barely escaped as a child?" he would ask his audience. "Newcomers they were not," Joseph would say, bringing the story to a close, "but strangers they remained."

And so, Joseph managed Beth Abraham's relationship with the police and all the local politicians. The mayor, city councilors, the school superintendent would all call him to express condolences when any tragedy involving Jews occurred, as if he was the High Priest. It was Joseph who would review the High Holiday security plan in great detail with Chief of Police Cal Thicke when the season cycled around. It was Joseph who continued to consult with Thicke regularly in the face of heightened concern and determine what additional security Beth Abraham needed.

When Vivian had asked Joseph about attending the forum, he mentioned that he did not have the time. *But you always make time for Cal Thicke*, she thought.

Vivian knew there were other ways to navigate city politics, relationships to build that need not be activated only around Beth Abraham's self-interested concerns. From a distance, she had seen interfaith collaboration as she pursued her crush in New York. Clergy from Christian, Jewish and Muslim congregations. Black people, Brown people, White people, working-class and affluent, all leveraging their resources to wage a shared fight. And they had won, sometimes.

Although she had considered other jobs coming out of rabbinical school—at smaller or less traditional synagogues, with less red tape, with fewer Will Goulds—Vivian had seen potential at Beth Abraham, a mid-sized congregation in a mid-sized city at a time of great-sized change.

Onstage, at the front of the sanctuary, the candidates settled into their seats and their congenial expressions. Farah and Sally sat down with their fellow congregants, and Vivian slipped into the row behind them just as the program began.

The forum was moderated by Trevor Almond, a local public-radio personality who worshipped at St. James. "Good evening, Providence," Almond began. "Thank you, St. James, for hosting this important event. Democracy matters these days, folks, especially in special elections, which have lower expected turnouts. And so, it is good to see that you, communities of faith, are ready to meet our candidates for mayor and engage with them on issues of great import. Tonight is about them getting to know you, and you getting to know them. Each candidate will take a few minutes to introduce themselves and their platforms, and then we will open it up to your questions for the rest of our time together."

Mike McCann was up first. He shifted around in his chair, trying to find the right position. He spoke about growing up working-class in Providence; about his leadership in the building trades union; about his service as a city councilor; and then about his few months, by luck of the draw, as mayor pro tem. To Vivian, he seemed well trained by seasoned political operatives who had helped him climb up the union ranks. His stint as mayor had certainly improved his posture and presence...or, at least, that's what the profile in the *Chronicle* said.

When it came to his platform, McCann followed the rules: Always bring it back to good jobs. Praise developers as job creators. Make vague but grand statements about being a city that can build opportunity for all.

Margaret Heath followed. She cited her credentials, her decades of fighting for equity. She referred to two important cases enforcing protections against housing discrimination which she had argued and won at the State Supreme Court. She highlighted that she could be both pragmatic and fiery, depending on what a given situation required. She closed with a vision for more diverse neighborhoods with more affordable housing and a Providence that remained open to all: people of color, immigrants, young people moving to town seeking opportunity.

Alex Santiago went last. He shared the story of immigrating with his parents from the Dominican Republic at age three, and what it was like to grow up on the south side of the city in an under-resourced school district. He discussed his plans to reduce the city's allocation of funds to the police department, which immigrant residents, Black residents, and other residents of color deeply distrusted to keep them safe. Rather, Santiago would invest in public schooling and affordable housing by increasing the number of rental vouchers available for low-income families.

Wearing jeans and a black t-shirt displaying a raised fist, he lacked the polished sheen of a typical politician, but, to Vivian, he came off as honest and effective in conveying his message. Given the city demographics—growing numbers of voters were people of color, immigrants, and/or young transplants—he was becoming a potential contender. But, as the local media liked to point out, Alex Santiago did not seem to care much about fundraising, so neither McCann nor Heath saw him as a threat.

While listening to the opening statements, Vivian scanned the crowd. Some members of the audience had donned paraphernalia pledging their allegiance. The McCann supporters, who sported buttons with the motto "McCann Can!" were primarily middle-aged, middle-class, and White. Those wearing "Vote Heath—Providence for Everyone" stickers were more of a mix, including young White moms in yoga pants and older people of color, with some of the latter sporting tenant union buttons as well. Santiago's people, who were button-less and sticker-less, were clearly the twenty-somethings wearing what twenty-somethings wear.

The first audience question, from a White parent with a McCann button, was about classroom size. Santiago discussed the opportunity gaps between White kids and Black, Latinx, and Asian kids in the city. McCann praised the school system, the teachers, the administrators, the janitors, then talked vaguely about collaboration and shared goals. Heath also praised the school system and proceeded to focus on how, in next year's budget process, the city could free up dollars to hire more teachers.

"Damn," whispered the young woman sitting next to Vivian. She had short blonde hair, long, crossed legs, and a power suit. Her blazer announced, "McCann Can!" Vivian peered over at the neat and quick notes she was jotting down on a lined pad. *Heath: more measured responses. Need more counterpunches.*

The next question came from a middle-aged Black woman. She shared that her son had recently been stopped by a policeman for no good reason for the third time in a few years. These incidents were taking their toll on him and many Black families in the city. "How will you make sure my kid, *our* kids," turning around to point to the small contingent of Black attendees, "are not harassed, or even killed, by the police?"

The woman in the suit pulled out her phone and began texting ferociously. It seemed peculiar that she should be a McCann supporter. Vivian could hear her whispering to herself as she typed. *Praise police. But not too much. Ensure all residents feel protected. Community task force.*

Margaret Heath answered first, speaking of the need for meaningful reforms: requiring that police officers intervene when witnessing egregious use of force, establishing independent oversight of the department, recruiting more police officers of color in order to reflect the city's demographics.

Then it was McCann's turn. "Thank you for your question.

I am sorry that happened to your son, but—uh, I mean, *and*— the police have one of the hardest jobs in this city, trying to keep us all safe." This line generated a few snickers, ruffling McCann. "We are going to look into our policies to, uh, ensure the best security for all our residents. There's always room for improvement. If elected, I want to invite interested residents to join a community task force so we can hear more directly from all of you."

The woman who asked the question grunted her disapproval at McCann's answer into the audience microphone. Vivian's neighbor continued scribbling, though these notes were too messy for Vivian to make out without her peeking getting obvious.

There was a heaviness in the air. Santiago let it linger. Then he shared his own run-ins with police, followed by his policy proposals: weeding out racist cops and reallocating the most recent increase of the police budget to underfunded schools, healthcare programs and housing for low-income residents.

As the conversation turned to a question about pensions, the air in the room seemed to thin, to soften. Vivian could not contain her curiosity. She leaned over to her neighbor. "I wouldn't have taken you for a McCann supporter."

"Sorry to disappoint you, but I am," the woman replied, with a hint of exasperation in her voice.

"And why is that?"

"I work for him," she said, looking back down at her notes.

"Hmm. Interesting," Vivian said. "Hi. I'm Vivian."

"Karla Dixon," the woman said, looking up. "Mike McCann's deputy campaign manager." She reached out her hand.

Vivian extended hers to complete the handshake. Perhaps

it was the sighs they had shared during some of the previous responses, or her haircut on the blurry border between queer and professional, but something about Karla made Vivian feel like they were more similar than Karla's button let on.

"Your boss's answer to that police question seemed like a dodge to me," she said.

"Yeah, well," Karla whispered, "when your base is union folks and older White Democrats it all comes down to maintaining the status quo while peppering in some vague statements about diversity that won't actually threaten it."

"Wow, that's pretty honest," Vivian said.

Karla sighed. "I'm sorry. I don't know why I said that, at least out loud. It's been a long day, a long week actually."

"I can imagine. Your campaign seems to be walking a tight rope," Vivian said, trying to sound schooled in the politics of Providence.

"New England certainly has a weird brand of liberal. I'm from Virginia, and there, all these Democrats would lose no sleep at night just calling themselves Republicans. You know," Karla said, cupping her mouth, "I really don't know why I'm unloading on you like this. Here's the thing. McCann's a good guy. He's still working on his execution and message, but he's a hard worker and wants good things for this city. He even started to do some of them when he was mayor pro tem.

"He grew up here, knows everyone from the guys working down at the hardware store to the police chief to the developers. He's got a good, reliable team, and we are going to ensure smart growth over the next four years. All right, back on message, so you want a sticker?"

"I'm still making up my mind, but that was a good sell at the end there." Vivian turned her attention back to the program. One of her congregants, Jerry Barnett, was standing in front of the microphone. In her experience, Jerry was reasonable about half the time. Vivian sunk in her seat, anticipating that this question might fall into the unreasonable half.

"Hate crimes against Jews have been on the rise," Jerry said, speaking loudly, as if there were no amplification device in front of him. "Last year, eleven people were brutally murdered by an antisemite in a synagogue a few hundred miles from here. And there have been threats made to Jewish communities all over the country. My mother survived the Holocaust and came to America seeking freedom and safety. She would turn over in her grave if she saw what was going on today. We've got to also be talking about protecting Jews, you know, assigning more police to protect our synagogues and community centers. What will you do to curb growing antisemitism?"

Vivian held her breath, sensing that Jerry's question fell somewhere in the middle of the spectrum she had constructed in her mind. The candidates all looked flustered by the question. No one jumped to answer. Karla texted some notes to McCann. Now that they were turned toward each other, Vivian could easily make out what she was typing. *Don't say too much, just go with platitudes.*

Heath sat up straight and pulled the microphone close to her mouth. She said that she would work with the Jewish community to better understand the threats and figure out how to deploy resources appropriately.

Santiago spoke next, his eyebrows inching closer and closer

to each other. "Sir, I'm sorry all that happened. But it's important to understand the different levels of threat in our city and make decisions based on who's getting beat up and killed.

"These threats you're talking about, they haven't materialized here, and you walk around this city with white skin. More police will mean more suspicion, more violence against people who look like me. We have to be careful and think of strategies that don't protect some while creating problems for others." The pews creaked with discomfort, including the one right in front of Vivian, where her congregants were sitting.

McCann leaned in to offer his response. "Well, uh, from my work on the city council, and in my time as mayor, I've known some great Jews in city government, so I think, with their support, we'll be able to work together to ensure that you all feel safe here."

Karla covered and rubbed her eyes. Vivian could only make out one phrase from the messy notes Karla was writing in response. *Work on the Jewish question.*

"That's going to take some cleaning up," Vivian said, leaning over toward Karla. "Say, has McCann spoken at any synagogues yet?"

"Is this a hypothetical question?" Karla said, still scribbling.

"I'm a rabbi at one, and it seems like it would do some good for all the candidates to talk more directly with Jewish voters." Vivian leaned in closer and continued, "If it makes you feel any better, the guy who asked the question is my congregant, so I guess we both have some work to do." Though Vivian did not quite know what work she was referring to.

"Back up." Karla said, raising her head and looking more

animated. "You're a rabbi?" Karla did a casual scan of Vivian. "Um, you really don't look like one."

"You know, everyone I meet who's over seventy says that too, so it's nice to have some variety," Vivian said half-joking, half-revealing her frustration.

"I'm sorry, it's just, well, you certainly don't look like the old geezer in the temple where I went to Hebrew school," Karla said, recovering. Vivian detected a bit of flirtation in Karla's response, but could not tell if that undertone was just part of the nature of digging oneself out of a hole.

"And to your question," Karla continued, "We'll go any-where. It's always good to talk to new groups. It's pretty clear Mike's got work to do to reach demographics outside of his immediate base. I'd just have to check our schedule to see when we could fit it in."

The last question came from an older White woman with no clear allegiance. A quarter of the houses on her block were being renovated, and she was worried about her property taxes going up so high that she would be forced to leave. "What will you do to reduce skyrocketing housing costs?"

McCann, to no one's surprise, felt that "ensuring smart growth" was the answer, as it would produce more market-rate housing and require good construction jobs to build them. Heath added that she would work for more city investment in subsidized housing and continue to address racist housing practices.

"Homeownership is one of the largest indicators of wealth that families can pass along to their kids," Santiago said, round-ing out the responses. "The rate of Black homeownership in

Providence is incredibly low. But that is what we need to get to the starting line. That is what equity looks like, and that is what I will fight for." He settled back into his chair, seemingly done. But suddenly his face lit up, and he leaned forward again.

"And let me tell you something," he continued. "You think Black folks are the ones living off of government welfare? Take a look at the deals the city cuts with developers for new luxury housing projects, and you'll see who's really feeding off the government. If elected, I'd make sure that they put in their fair share to the public pot."

Karla leaned over to Vivian. "Wrong crowd for that answer."

"Though Santiago's certainly making this a more intriguing race," Vivian said. "You can't argue with that."

"Sure," Karla said. "But who in your synagogue would vote for him?"

Vivian shrugged her shoulders and angled herself away from Karla, toward the front. *No one,* she thought.

Trevor Almond closed the forum with a few announcements, encouraging everyone to vote in June.

"Time for some damage control, Rabbi," Karla said, handing Vivian her card. "Give me a call and we'll set something up. It would be good for Mike."

"And it would be good for my members to get more connected to what's happening in their own backyard," Vivian said. Karla was rising to leave as Vivian added, "Even if it makes us both squirm."

Karla looked back at her with a half-smile that was hard to decipher. Vivian could not tell if she was communicating mutual understanding or an indication that Vivian had read her totally wrong. But something had compelled Vivian to overshare, too, to spill her most private thoughts.

EIGHT

A FTER GREETING HER other congregants, Vivian shuffled out of the pew, hoping to introduce herself to the candidates. McCann seemed busy with supporters and staff members, including Karla. She saw an opening to talk to Margaret Heath, who had just finished a conversation with some audience members, and approached her.

Vivian noticed in their conversation that Heath looked right at her, with warm green eyes surrounded by smile wrinkles, rather than around her at all the other people she could have been mingling with instead. In an effort to pique Heath's interest, Vivian mentioned that Beth Abraham was considering what to do with their vacant land.

"The city could certainly use some more affordable or mixed-income housing," Heath said. "We are working on some better incentives for property owners to charge at or below market rate. If I'm elected, your congregation should pursue them."

After taking Health's business card, Vivian looked over at Alex Santiago. As she was contemplating what she could say, Heather greeted her from behind.

"Nice turnout, Viv! So, you think your congregants are ready to fight the good fight for justice now?"

"It was a start," Vivian said, responding to Heather's sarcasm with some sincerity. "How'd you think that went overall?"

"Oh, you know, same old song and dance," Heather said. "A bit more interesting this time around. Santiago mixes things up. And man, McCann is really not the sharpest crayon in the box. The real question, though, is who is that woman you were chatting with in the pews?"

"McCann's deputy campaign manager," Vivian said.

"Seriously? I thought she was your date or something."

Vivian smiled. "She seemed…interesting."

"You totally like her!" Heather looked in Karla's direction.

Vivian grabbed Heather's arm. "Heather, don't look!"

"Did you tell her you're a rabbi?" Heather asked. Vivian nodded.

"How'd that land?"

"The usual."

"Well, it's not like politics is such a normal gig," Heather laughed. "So maybe you've met your match."

Vivian rolled her eyes. "Seems a bit early to make that call."

Sally and Farah walked over and signaled that they were

ready to go. Vivian hugged Heather and began heading toward
the exit. She wanted to talk to Karla again, but she appeared
too busy chatting with other people in power suits. Vivian
wracked her brain for a convincing excuse: follow up about a
key issue, remind her about coming to Beth Abraham. None
seemed right. But Vivian could at least test if they both felt it,
the intrigue, before leaving.

Vivian noticed a congregant of hers standing directly in
Karla's line of vision. With Farah and Sally in tow, Vivian initiated a quick hello. She then found herself stuck in a conversation about Geraldine's vacation to Florida. Luckily, the other
two could do most of the talking. As Geraldine was regaling
them with tales of whatever it is older Jews do in Florida in the
winter, Vivian could feel Karla's gaze on her. She glanced back a
few times. Finally, their eyes met. They both held the stare. And
Vivian felt a current shoot through her body.

But there was nothing more to do about it that night. They
were minding their own politics. As soon as Vivian could tear
Sally and Farah away from Geraldine, she left the church, wondering if Karla was watching her as she walked away.

. . .

"I can't believe what the Black guy said in response to Jerry's
question," Sally said on their ride home. "I mean, does he even
know our history? Or read the news?"

"Maybe he was just flustered," Farah said. "But it does seem
like he needs to brush up on persecution in the 20th century."

Vivian saw an opening, to start to untangle the knot of

antisemitism, of their privilege, of...she could not make out all
of the threads just yet. "It may help for him to know more about
our history, but I think when Jerry spoke, Santiago just saw him
as another White man."

"But he's obviously Jewish." Sally said.

"I'm not sure if everyone sees those as different," Vivian
said.

"Well, those people are ignorant."

"I think some of them are just focused on other things,
other threats," Vivian said, "and don't interact much with Jewish people."

"And whose fault is that?" Sally asked.

"One culprit has been segregation, in neighborhoods, in
schools." Vivian questioned her answer. *This, now,* she thought,
is why I'm here, at Beth Abraham. And yet instead of feeling grat-
ified, she felt unsure where to begin, as if she were staring at a
page of Talmud without knowing Aramaic.

"Given that there wasn't time for a whole history lesson,"
Sally said, "he just seemed antisemitic to me."

"We all know we're voting for Heath anyway, so what does
it matter?" Farah spoke up.

Vivian took the question seriously. "It matters if we want to
be involved in the life of our city," she said, sitting up straighter
in her seat, planting her feet firmly on the car floor. "And if
the candidates don't know how to engage with our community, then we need to do a better job building relationships with
them, and with—"

"We do, though," Sally interrupted. "Politicians come and
speak to us on Holocaust Remembrance Day every year."

"But I'm talking about the fate of all of Providence," Vivian said, "not just our Jewish community. Some of our kids are in the public schools. Our housing costs are going up too. We also have a real stake in these other issues."

"I'll give you that," Sally said. "My property taxes have gone through the roof over the past few years."

"We are residents of Providence, not just Jews of Providence," Vivian said. "If we took that seriously, maybe Alex Santiago's answer, or McCann's answer, to Jerry's question would have been different." She continued in a lower voice, "Heck, maybe Jerry's question would have been different."

They pulled up to Sally's house "All right, Rabbi," she said. "Thanks for the ride. It was an interesting night. And hey, maybe if we had better relationships, we could convince the church to serve better snacks. Crackers, cheese and coffee? How unsatisfactory."

Farah laughed. "And how goyish!"

NINE

ON HIS WAY HOME from Beth Abraham on the East Side, the White side, Raymond unwound against the backdrop of the setting spring sun, singing aloud to the Earth, Wind & Fire CD on heavy rotation in his car.

The hours he had clocked at the synagogue over the past two decades were long, especially when keeping the building open for all those evening meetings that, judging by the speed with which participants raced out afterward, were none too dear to anyone. But Raymond enjoyed his drives home at night, when there was no traffic, and when he was free from the complicated world of his work.

He tapped the steering wheel with his thumbs. "Do you

remember," he belted out, "the twenty-first night of September?" Raymond turned onto his street. Phillips Lane had been a predominantly Black and Latinx block for decades, but it was changing rapidly.

A few weeks before, flyers had mysteriously appeared on doorsteps offering good money for people's homes. Young, White couples were moving in...to the house two doors down, the one down the street, and the one by the convenience store, which itself was rumored to be turning into a fair-trade coffee shop. There was already a dog-grooming business around the block. What's next? he wondered. Four-dollar, fair-trade coffee *for dogs*?

These changes had turned the previously mindless routine of parking into a frustrating challenge, especially when he arrived home later in the evening. Raymond did a few laps around his block before settling for a spot two streets away. Rubbing the small of his back, which had been acting up, he got out of his car and headed toward the house.

It was a yellow triple-decker that he and his wife, Sheila, had purchased seventeen years earlier with their life savings and a low-interest loan. Every time he returned home, a scene or two from that first day flitted across his mind's eye: shifting the furniture around and experimenting with different layouts; tripping on his son's toy construction truck as he brought in another set of boxes, causing him a subtle limp that lasted for weeks; introducing himself to his neighbors to delay more unpacking. "It was the happiest day of my life," he would tell Sheila, who would roll her eyes. But he still repeated it. Over and over.

Raymond noticed that a few of the Black-eyed Susans they had planted close to the sidewalk were trampled on. He bent down, trying to ignore the pain in his back, and lifted the flowers back to their original posture. As Raymond mirrored their poses, one held its shape, but the others flopped back downward.

"Hey, sweetie," Sheila shouted from the kitchen as he hung his jacket up on the hook next to the door. He followed the sound of her voice. She was washing dishes in the sink.

"There's still some spaghetti and meatballs for you on the stove," she said as Raymond wrapped his arms around her waist and kissed her cheek. "It might be cold." Still scrubbing and facing the sink, she asked, "How was your day, hun?"

"Same old, same old," Raymond said, as he detached himself from Sheila and walked over to the oven. He unfurled the pasta onto his plate, and scraped the meat sauce out of the pan, pouring it onto the noodles. "Where's Mac?"

"Just missed him," Sheila said. "He went over to Freddie's to play video games or something."

Raymond, still standing up, took a few bites. As he shoved the fork into his mouth, a few ribbons of spaghetti fell to the ground. "Oops!"

Sheila turned from the sink and spotted the result of her husband's clumsiness. "I just cleaned everything up, and you have to go and make a whole new mess." She wet a paper towel, and before bending down to clean, shoved Raymond lightly toward the kitchen table. He surrendered and sat down. He ate in silence as Sheila cleaned up the small splatter of red on the wooden floor.

"Aren't you going to ask me how my day was?" Sheila asked, throwing the crumpled paper towel into the garbage.

"Of course. I'm sorry, baby. And how was your day?"

"Saw about ten patients without any break, but nothing

more serious or difficult than usual." Sheila worked as a nurse at a nearby health clinic. She had started her career in the emergency room, but she had transitioned to the clinic to make the juggle of all of her responsibilities more manageable.

"Also, Cassandra let me know about a job opening at Morris's work," she added, returning to the sink to wash the last of the dinner dishes. "Better hours. It's closer to home." Sheila had been on Raymond's case for years about finding a new job.

But Raymond was a creature of habit. His routines were in his bones. He ate the same breakfast every day: a cheese biscuit and orange juice in his bright green Boston Celtics mug. He left home each day at 9:30, skipping the worst of the morning traffic. He knew the ins and outs of Congregation Beth Abraham as well as he knew his red eighteen-year-old Ford Expedition (which he'd bought only after his '81 red Expedition bit the dust).

She turned off the faucet. "Come on, Ray." Sheila said, putting the last plate in the dishrack. "I want to have dinner with my husband." Every few months, they replayed this exact conversation. She kissed the top of his head without lingering and turned toward the living room.

"Isn't this the part where you bring up my father?" Raymond said, circling his plate with his fork. Myron Weeks also had had a propensity to miss family dinners. He had been active in voter registration campaigns when Raymond was growing up. Raymond's friends had all looked up to Myron, or as they called him, Mr. Weeks. But Raymond felt more longing than pride when he thought about his father.

"Seems like I don't need to," Sheila sighed, exiting the kitchen.

TEN

"GRANDPA, GRANDPA! Can I have more ice cream?"

"No, Ryan. Everybody gets one scoop," Joseph said.

"But I didn't eat my ice cream last time because I was sick," Ryan cried, banging on the kitchen table.

"No."

"But what about half a scoop?"

"No!" Joseph said, raising his voice, as he stacked the empty cups.

"But Grandpa, today Caleb hit me in school and it hurt a lot. And ice cream would make me feel better."

Joseph turned his back to Ryan, placing the dishes in the sink. He closed his eyes, completing his breath with a grunt.

How did a six-year-old know how to negotiate, manipulate even?

Joseph and his wife, Miriam, were babysitting, while their son and daughter-in-law went out to see a play. Joseph loved his grandson dearly, but often judged his son and daughter-in-law's parenting as too lenient.

As Joseph surrendered and served Ryan another scoop of ice cream, he looked at Miriam with tired eyes.

"Don't read too much into this, Joseph. It's just ice cream," she warned.

"Miriam, it's never just ice cream," he said, rejoining her at the table adorned with plaid wool placemats. "How come they don't teach him to honor his elders? How come they don't create a distinction between the holy and the ordinary? How come they don't send their son to Jewish day school?"

"They've made their choices, Joseph," Miriam said. "We taught Jake to do just that. And he's made good choices. Audrey is such a strong woman, and a good mother."

"He was such a good davvener, Miriam. He could have carried a whole community on his wings during the High Holidays. He was destined to—"

"Joseph, it's just ice cream," Miriam said, rising to return the soggy container to the freezer. "Get over it, go write a sermon or take a walk. Maybe you should try yoga one of these days. It seems to calm a lot of people down."

Joseph grumbled and folded his arms, unsure of his next move. The landline rang.

"Hello?" Joseph said, retrieving the cordless phone, pleased with the prospect of distraction.

"Hiya, Rabbi, it's Will Gould."

"Will. Nice to hear from you." Joseph gulped. Will only called to announce a big donation or ask him for a favor, and since he had recently gifted Beth Abraham $30,000, Joseph could sense which side of the scale this call would land on. "How are you?"

"Doing well. Business is good. Fiona just got into Yale. So now that'll be three generations!"

"Mazel tov!" Joseph said, though his face did not match his exclamation. All he could think about were these silly names: Fiona, Ryan. Why do so many Jews cut themselves off from the tradition?

"Thank you, Rabbi."

"So, what can I do for you?" Joseph asked, walking with the phone out of the kitchen. "I haven't seen you around shul much these days."

"Working eighty hours a week just doesn't leave much time for shul, you know?"

"Of course, of course." Joseph thought about his father, who had worked eighty, sometimes ninety hours a week to put food on the table when he came to the United States, and who had still kept Shabbat. He had even managed to chant half the parsha in his synagogue most weeks.

"I want to talk to you about the parcel of vacant land that Beth Abraham owns," Will said. "I'd like to make an offer."

Joseph sank down into the leather couch in the dimly-lit living room. "The board has been considering some options. Some members are in talks with the bank about investing in a small residential community for Jewish seniors."

"Rabbi, that plan has been in the works for years. Has there been any movement?" Will said, rhetorically. "Sounds like a lot of work, and a lot of investment. I can take that land off your hands for a good price. And it'll still be under tribal ownership." Will tittered at his own joke.

"You know, Will, I don't make the decisions here."

"But people listen to you," Will said. "They respect you."

Respect? Joseph thought. *Like how three-fourths of the congregation only interact with me when someone dies or they want to lower the expectations for their child's bar or bat mitzvah? Like how the ritual committee decides to overrule me and cancel services on the second day of Shavuot?*

"What are you offering, Will?" Joseph asked hesitantly, wondering if now was the time to indulge his curiosity or if he should just direct Will to Harry, as he knew protocol demanded.

"1.5 million dollars."

Joseph coughed. "Just for the land?"

"Yes, Rabbi." The number of times Will said "Rabbi" in this conversation annoyed Joseph. It was as though Will was soothing him into thinking that he had power, when they both knew the truth. "I want to take care of my community. And I know it would help given that membership is declining."

"You've been talking to Harry?"

"Oh, you know, here and there." Joseph could hear Will's smile over the phone.

"But not at shul." Joseph knew that little punch was the only victory he would have to hold onto after this call. "Why don't you send Harry a proposal for the board to consider?"

"I'll do that, Rabbi," Will said. "And you just think about

what the shul could do with that extra pocket change." Joseph hung up and dropped the phone at his side.

Miriam had followed Joseph into the living room. "So, which is worse? Getting handled by a six-year-old or by Will Gould?"

Joseph closed his eyes and sank back into the couch. He raised his head and arms to the ceiling, as if pleading with God. That...or resting in Warrior Pose.

ELEVEN

W HEN SHE WAS not brunching with Lisa and Heather, Vivian frequented her favorite bookstore, a few blocks from her apartment, on her day off. She began her routine with a latte purchased from Once Upon a Book's in-store café, and then she read the newspaper headlines: first from the *Times*, then from the *Chronicle*.

On this day, one in particular stood out. "McCann in Deep Water Amid Union Corruption Revelations." The article reported that during McCann's tenure leading the building trades union, the union had hired a crooked lawyer who used threatening tactics in contract negotiations.

Vivian thought of Karla. Her mind often drifted toward

Karla these days. After they met, Vivian had emailed and called to set up a time for McCann to visit Beth Abraham. But Karla had not gotten back to her.

Vivian filed away her disappointment and found comfort in the scent of coffee and new books. She was historically a devoted nonfiction reader but had recently gotten on a kick of reading mysteries. As she picked up different novels, none of which piqued her interest, she noticed the profile of a woman who looked a lot like Karla a few rows away. The electric current that had run through her body at the church returned. Could that really be her?

She dropped down into the aisle. Staring from behind the bookcase of mystery novels, Vivian hesitated to determine her next move. The woman turned in her direction, and Vivian saw that Maybe-Karla was definitely Karla, ever in a power suit, with a Bluetooth in her ear.

Vivian walked as casually as she could to the poetry section to get a better look and strategize about what she would say. She noticed that Karla was browsing in the political philosophy section. Bingo! This was homefield advantage for Vivian, who had studied political science in college. Karla flipped through Marx's *Capital*. Vivian stood up, resolute in a power pose, and willed herself to walk over.

Her heart was pounding. She supposed everyone in the store could hear it. She planted herself next to Karla and leaned in. "Didn't take you for a Marxist."

Karla was surprised but seemingly happy to see Vivian when she turned. "You know, I've dabbled," Karla said, closing the book and putting it back on the shelf, "but I'm just too attached to my iPhone and reliable garbage pickup to fully subscribe." Vivian was impressed, and intimidated, by Karla's wit. But she could handle this.

"Karla, right?" Vivian asked, as if she had not been constantly saying her name and seeing her face in her mind.

"Right, hi. It's nice to see you again, Vivian. I owe you an email."

The charge came back when Karla said her name.

"It's fine. It must be a pretty busy time." Affirming, always affirming. Vivian wondered if she should take a stronger position.

"Well, that, yes, and we've had to deal with some unexpected sh...obstacles."

"Seems like the union ties are backfiring," Vivian said.

"Seems like you read the newspaper next to your Torah at the breakfast table," Karla said, looking toward the shelf and picking up another large book.

"You know, rabbis don't actually read the Torah while eating breakfast. Well, some might, but I'd prefer some Rawls," Vivian said, pointing to the volume Karla had just chosen. Two could play this game.

"Mike is getting a reputation for not being well rounded enough in some of his speaking engagements, mostly with the richer crowds. And some donors. So, it's my job to get him up to speed."

"By having a book club over a six-hundred-page treatise on liberal political philosophy?" Vivian said.

"By subtly keeping a book in plain sight that'll score him some extra points, and then sprinkling in some good one-liners from it," Karla said, flipping through the book.

"So, it's a prop?"

"Something like that," Karla said, managing to be both embarrassed and flirtatious at once.

"Again, you're not making the best case for your guy."

"Look," Karla said, walking toward the register as Vivian followed, "I believe Mike has the relationships to get things done and sometimes shift a little to the left: balance the budget, get some market-rate housing built instead of just luxury, and keep some of the businesses that are currently threatening to leave town. Margaret Heath talks a good game, I'll admit. But she can't make it happen. Centrism is the best way to get things done." Karla's voice strained on the last sentence, as if she did not fully believe it. She recovered with a smile. "You may not get it, since the prophets weren't exactly centrists, from what I remember."

"Ah, yes, your adventures at Hebrew school," Vivian said, raising one eyebrow. She settled in beside Karla behind a few other customers waiting to check out.

"Good memory."

"You know," Vivian said, "the Judaism that I subscribe to is actually all about finding the middle ground in unideal situations. The rabbis, who are really the forebears of what we do and believe today, had to come up with a whole new blueprint after the world of the prophets and the priests was destroyed. After the Jews were dispersed, our ancestors constantly had to establish new laws and customs in order to adapt to their new reality, while maintaining their Jewish identity and sense of—"

Vivian stopped. "Oh my God, I really didn't mean to do that."

"What?" Karla said, laughing. "Give a sermon in the bookstore checkout line to a lapsed Jew? I have to say, it was intriguing, Rabbi. Almost intriguing enough to get me to come back to synagogue after two decades. Almost."

"I appreciate you making light of it," Vivian said, "but you have to admit, what I did there is just a totally strange way of interacting."

"I'm in politics, Vivian. You could add a subtle segue to a position on affordable housing and end with a 'That's why you should vote for me!' and I wouldn't blink."

"Yeah, but…" Vivian was losing momentum, frustrated at herself for embodying the assumptions she tried to defeat.

"Next!" the cashier said, looking at Karla.

"I got to go. But call our scheduler, Jeff, tomorrow," Karla said, handing Vivian another business card. "We just hired him so I can actually do my real job. He'll find a time that works in the next few weeks for Mike to come by your synagogue. It's a crazy time, but this is important to us. And he'll be there, John Rawls and all."

Trying to regain some boldness, and channeling what she thought a normal person flirting might say, Vivian responded, "And how about you?"

Karla smiled. "Yes, I'll be there too. You may even get a photo op with me and a Torah."

TWELVE

"I SAW KARLA TODAY," Vivian told Heather as they stood in the popcorn line. They were about to see a raunchy comedy with a full female cast in a theater a few towns over, where they were less likely to run into congregants.

"Karla...? Karla! The hottie from the mayor's forum!"

"That's right," Vivian said, wincing at Heather's description.

"What happened?"

"We were in a bookstore."

Heather chuckled. "Typical."

Unfazed by Heather's mocking, Vivian continued. "I went over to her and struck up a conversation. There was some flirtatious banter. I did that thing where I nervously start to give a sermon about my foundational beliefs about Judaism. Then she said that McCann would come to speak at the synagogue and that she'd come too."

"And?" Heather said. Vivian shrugged her shoulders. "That's it?" Heather continued, wanting more. "Is there a date, is there a plan? Where did you leave things?"

"I guess we'll have to wait and see."

"Viv," Heather said, resting her hand on Vivian's shoulder. "I think you should be bold here. You like her. You've gotten some good vibes. Just ask her out!"

"I'll think about it," Vivian said, moving closer to the register as the line shortened.

"Come on, what would Moses do?"

Vivian looked at Heather blankly.

"Miriam? Heschel? Um…Ruth Bader Ginsburg?" Heather added. Still no response. "So that's not a thing for you guys?"

"Nope," Vivian said. "We have too much anxiety and too many opinions. Decisiveness does not run through our veins."

Heather rolled her eyes at Vivian. They each ordered a bag of popcorn topped with a drizzle of butter.

As they made their way to the correct theater, passing posters for upcoming releases and scrolling through their emails for just another minute, Heather halted. Vivian stopped and looked behind her when she noticed Heather not matching her pace.

"Do you have Karla's number?" Heather asked.

"I got it when I met her."

"Why don't you just call her right now? I'm here to support you, pump you up."

"I can't do that, Heather."

"Yes, you can. You do hard things all the time, Viv."

Vivian stood in silence, hunched over her phone, avoiding Heather's gaze. Heather suddenly reached over and stripped Vivian's phone from her, navigating right to her contacts.

"What are you doing?" Vivian asked.

"I'm doing you a favor."

Vivian tried to get the phone back, but Heather kept her at a distance with one hand while continuing to search with the other.

"Karla Dixon. Aha!" Heather immediately pressed the call button. She handed the phone back to Vivian who let out a sharp shriek and pressed the red hang-up icon.

"Well, now what's she going to think?" Heather said, looking very pleased with herself.

"I. Can't. Believe. You. Did. That," Vivian said, looking around the theater hallway to see if anyone was watching them.

"You might as well try again since the call registered on her phone," Heather said.

Vivian let out a deep breath. "Fine." Breathing heavily, she walked over to an empty corner and finally pressed the call button. Heather followed.

It rang once. Then twice. Vivian was hoping with all her being Karla would not pick up.

"Hello?" she heard on the other side of the line.

"Oh, um, hi. It's Vivian Green, Rabbi Vivian."

She slapped her hand against her head. *Rabbi Vivian?*

"Oh, hi."

"I know you're pretty busy and that I'll be calling Jeff to

schedule a time for Mike to come to the synagogue, but, in the meantime, I was hoping we could meet up. I'd, um, I'd love to learn more about the political landscape here, and, well, after running into you today, I realized you were the right person." Vivian's whole body was tight.

"Uh, let me look at my schedule."

There was a long silence over the phone. Vivian turned her body away from Heather. Presumably, Karla was looking through her schedule on her phone, but all Vivian could think was that she was wondering why this weirdo rabbi had called.

"I'm booked solid until nine for the next three weeks," Karla said. "But we could get a drink after nine sometime."

"That works for me," Vivian said, even though she preferred to be in bed by ten thirty. "How about Ruby's?"

"The Kitchen Sink is more my speed," Karla said. "Plus, they sometimes give me free beer there."

Vivian wondered what about Karla's life led her to receive free beer. "Okay, how about Wednesday?" she asked.

"All right. Wednesday it is. See you then."

Vivian hung up, turned around and glared furiously at Heather, who had heard the whole conversation.

"Looks like you just set yourself up another night meeting!"

"Hey," Vivian said, holding her stare. "Given the situation you just put me in, I think I should get points for recovering."

"Fine, I'll give you a few points." Heather said, pumping her fist in the air. "You have a date, girl!"

"Oh my God," Vivian said, letting it sink in. "But do you think *she* thinks it's a date?"

"I don't know how you gays work," Heather said, as she

put her arm around Vivian's shoulders and guided her into the theater.

"That makes two of us."

THIRTEEN

WHEN RAYMOND OPENED the door after his ritual laps around the neighborhood in search of parking, his nineteen-year-old son Mac and several of his friends were splayed out on the sofas in the living room, shouting over one another. Raymond often returned to this scene in the evenings and did not think it warranted much engagement. He placed his keys on the hook next to the door and walked toward the kitchen.

As he passed his son, though, he noticed that Mac's right eye was swollen, his lip was cut and he was holding a patch of gauze on the back of his head.

"What's going on, boys?" Raymond interrupted, cutting through the tangle of voices.

Noticing his father for the first time, Mac looked up, straight at him. Raymond reached out to examine his son. "Pops, it was the damn cops again," Mac explained. The lingering sounds of the other boys' voices grew quiet. "I was riding my bike home from work," Mac continued. "I went through a red light and got pulled over by a cop. He gave me a ticket. On my bike!"

"Mac, you know that you're not supposed to—"

"Hold up. Let me finish."

Raymond's jaw clenched. He did not appreciate being interrupted by his son, but he let it pass this time, something he found himself doing more and more.

"Then this cop started searching me. No reason. He found some Advil in my pocket and called for backup. I told him what it was, just medicine for a headache. But he said he wasn't buying it. Told me to hold my hands up against the car."

Mac took another deep breath. "I hesitated, but I didn't even say anything! And he slammed my head in against the car. I hollered, and he did it again!" His voice got quieter. "When backup came, they took one look at the pills and knew it was just Advil. And the cop that stopped me said, 'This time, you can go.'"

Mac got up from the orange couch and started pacing. Raymond was silent. Mac filled in the void. "*This time*, I can go? I can fucking go? He left me with a bloody face!"

Mac's friend Greg spoke up. "Fuck the police. It's too much, Mr. Weeks!"

"We've got to challenge this," Freddie said. "File a complaint or something. Charge the guy with assault. Take him to court."

"That just means filing a complaint against a cop *with* a cop." Felix said, leaning back into the La-Z-Boy chair, crossing his legs. "They'll just protect each other."

"Hey Freddie," Greg asked, "Your cousin, he's running for mayor or something, right?"

"He sure is!" Freddie said. "And Alex is shouting from the rooftops about how the police are treating us, every chance he gets. Just like he did during those protests a while back."

"And what did those get us?" Felix asked.

Mac swatted his arms at the air. "Just more police on the street corners pushing us around, seems like."

"If Freddie's cousin is running for mayor and talking about this all over town," Greg said, "maybe people will start to listen. You know, maybe *White* people will start to listen."

The others laughed. Raymond focused on Mac's face and felt his own eyes moisten.

"You think our grandparents didn't try that?" Felix said.

Greg spoke through the laughs. "Freddie, why don't you talk to your cousin? See if he can help us sue the cop that beat Mac up."

"Whoa. What now?" Raymond interrupted. "Mac, you're not suing no one."

"Why not, Pops?" Now that Raymond was resisting, of course Mac would be warming to the idea. "White people sue all the time. You telling me I'm not as good as they are?" Mac let out a smile.

Raymond could see traces of his father's face in Mac's. In a way, Mac had been named for Myron Weeks. Though he had not been home very much when Raymond was a kid, every

Wednesday night, after working his factory job and the doors in his neighborhood, Myron would whip up his famous mac and cheese for dinner. Raymond had raised the possibility of naming their son after his own father's cooking as a joke in the delivery room. Sheila teared up at the memory of Myron, who had died a few years earlier. She loved it.

"You know," Freddie said, addressing his friends, "last time I saw Alex, he said they were trying to recruit more White people to use their money or relationships or whatever White people've got to help move public funds from the cops to things that could actually be good for us."

"We can work with that," Mac said, starting to pace again, getting more energized with each step. "Hey, Pops, how about all those White people you know from the synagogue? You think someone, Rabbi Joseph maybe, would sign onto something like that? You know, give us more credibility?"

"That's what I'm talking about!" Greg said.

"I don't know, man," Felix said. "Sounds about as inspired as when you tried to cook chili in my mom's waffle maker."

Raymond closed his eyes. He thought of something that had happened earlier that day, something that he would normally try to forget immediately. As kids were waiting for their parents after Beth Abraham's Hebrew school, he was entertaining some of them. It was part of his routine. He would roll a garbage can down the hallway while a few of the younger kids—regulars, who Raymond knew by name—chucked crumpled-up paper into it, like a basketball arcade game.

As Raymond feinted a quick left and then turned right with the garbage can, it collided with one of the moms, who had been texting on her phone while walking to her kid's classroom. She stumbled to the ground. Everyone in the hall heard the noise and turned and stared at Raymond, at the mother on the floor. She looked at him. The judgment, the coldness in her eyes, was more than Raymond could handle. He looked away.

Raymond regrouped, offered an apology and his hand, but she would not accept either. The rest of the crowd continued to stare. Raymond knew most of the faces. Some of them often asked how he was doing on their way out the door, without pausing to hear the answer. But Raymond had felt like an intruder in that moment, in that hallway. Even Avi and Micah, the two kids who played this game with him most days, had stepped back from him, avoiding eye contact and holding back nervous laughter.

"I don't know, Mac. I'll ask, but don't count on it," was all Raymond could muster.

"Come on, Pops. Work your magic," Mac said. "Those White people love you."

The rest of the group joined in Mac's appeal. "Come on, Mr. Weeks."

"Okay, okay. Hush. I'll try, Mac," Raymond said, rubbing his back. "I'll try."

FOURTEEN

VIVIAN ARRIVED AT The Kitchen Sink at five of nine, with a few minutes to catch her breath. She had come straight from a mourner's house.

Vivian deeply appreciated the direction provided by the customs of mourning in times of disarray: what to wear, how to sit, what to eat, when to pray, when to memorialize and when to start seeking out normal again.

The bar was mostly empty. The walls were wood, the light was dim. Vivian sat down at a table toward the back, under a painting of two skeletons in wedding garb getting into a Camaro with a "Just Married" sign on the rear bumper. She was wearing a black pencil skirt and a dark-green silk blouse. She still had not mastered professional footwear and was self-conscious of her slip-on flats, slightly too delicate to fit into the image and personality she wanted to convey. She had hoped to go home and change for this maybe-date, but she had stayed longer than expected at the Aronsons'.

As Vivian imagined what she would have preferred to be wearing, Karla appeared through the door with a pile of flyers in hand. She surveyed the room and noticed Vivian sitting in the back. Vivian waved. She wondered if her gesture was too vigorous. She decided to balance out the enthusiasm by not getting up to greet Karla. She thought it necessary to send mixed signals, in case this turned out not to be a date in Karla's mind.

"Where are you coming from?" Vivian asked. Karla, seemingly unconflicted about all the different greeting options, sat down.

"Doing some damage control on this union story. The fire's almost out, but the story won't die easily. Heath, in particular, won't let it go."

"Always putting out fires, huh?"

"That's politics," Karla said. "And how about you? Where are you coming from, Rabbi?"

Vivian hated when people jokingly called her "Rabbi," but she did not let on. "I was just at a mourner's house."

"Oh. Is that, uh, are you okay?"

"It's pretty normal. And I actually don't mind them. Sometimes, depending on how tragic the death is, supporting the family can be very draining. But Norma was ninety-six and died with her family around her and Frank Sinatra playing in the background. People have been coming by all week celebrating her life and sharing stories, remembering dirty jokes she used to tell on a loop when her memory started to go."

Karla snorted as she sipped her water. She recovered quickly, taking off her blazer and setting it on the chair behind her. "Wow, so you really are a rabbi. How did that happen?"

Vivian told Karla about how Judaism was in the air she breathed; about her mom; about Mimi, the badass rabbi of her college who'd brought her students along to protests against the Iraq war; about how much she wanted to be like Mimi, whose energy was supportive and strong.

The waiter approached them and greeted Karla by name. They ordered. A pale ale for Karla, a white wine for Vivian.

"Would you like any food, ladies?" he asked.

"I'm starving," Karla said, looking down at the black menu with white lettering. "I'll have the deluxe burger."

"Hmm." Vivian hummed as she quickly perused her options. She had not eaten dinner at the shiva house. (There was only so much apple kugel one could consume in a week.)

When she was not at a fully kosher restaurant, Vivian ate only vegetarian food. But the options here were slim: an uninspired salad and a veggie patty. She noticed that the fried chicken, however, was advertised with large font and labeled "Providence's best." Vivian's mouth watered.

She unfurled her napkin and released her utensils, even though she had no food yet. She worried about seeming indecisive. "I'll have the fried chicken," she said, in a raised voice. When the waiter left, Vivian continued to fidget with her fork.

"Take it easy, it's just dinner," Karla said.

"Actually, I don't usually eat meat or chicken that's not

kosher," Vivian explained, "but I allow myself two orders of fried chicken a year."

"Why two?" Karla asked.

"In Jewish tradition, doing something three times means that you've habituated yourself to it. So, for example, once you've started to pray every day for three days, it's as if you have taken on the obligation. I've decided that if I'm going to break the rules, I could inversely apply the same concept. If I only commit a sin twice in a set period of time, I haven't made it a habit."

"Uh, I'm not a great Jew," Karla said. "Hell, I don't know if I'd even call myself Jewish, but that doesn't sound kosher to me."

"Sure, it's not a position with 100% integrity, but there's just no good kosher fried chicken out there. And it's not like it's bacon. Or lobster!" Vivian subconsciously made her hands into lobster claws, noticed and secured them in her lap. "And I figure you won't judge."

"Your secret's safe with me."

"It's not a secret, it's just, um, Jewish legal gymnastics for the modern age."

Karla raised one eyebrow. "I'm pretty sure that's another way of saying secret."

Vivian could not read her reaction. Did Karla think she was weird? Crazy? Endearing?

Karla interrupted Vivian's internal monologue. "So, if I remember correctly, the premise of this meeting was to learn about the local political landscape. What do you want to know?"

Vivian herself had almost forgotten that particular premise and she was not feeling any urgency to get there.

"Yes, uh—well, first, how'd you end up doing what you're doing?" she asked. Karla paused. *Does she want to be here?* Vivian wondered. *Is she enjoying this conversation, this flow between what is work and what is personal?*

Then Karla told her about how she'd protested her college's investment in fossil fuels; how the tactics they used did not seem to lead anywhere; how her mom worked to secure better science education as a member of their local school committee; how the two fought over how change happened. At some point, Karla began to wonder what it all looked like through the eyes of decision makers, and she started working on electoral campaigns.

"So, what's your conclusion about how to bring about change?" Vivian asked.

"Well, Mike is a progressive at heart. He believes in democratizing city resources. But the jury's out on how far that belief can go. We crunched the actual numbers around a higher percentage of affordable housing units. Heath and Santiago talk a big game, but they're not realistic, they don't account for all the real costs."

Karla continued, "Heath was the lawyer on this deal for a big mixed-income project, the Hayward Houses, that the South Side CDC was in the process of closing a few months back."

Vivian remembered hearing about it. Bree, Lisa's partner, had worked on the project.

"Fifty percent of the units would have been affordable," Karla continued. "It would have been a great story: 'Black-led community developer sets new precedent for affordable housing.'" She raised her arm and mimed a newspaper headline. "But some of the public money fell through because of city budget cuts and dried-up federal loan programs. And without those funds, the project became untenable. So CK Construction scooped up the land they were planning to use. And the thing is, CK's project will generate a hell of a lot more income for other priorities in Providence as they start paying property taxes—for schools, services for seniors. So, you see, we can't just go scare off the developers with tighter constraints."

Their food arrived. Vivian immediately took a huge bite out of a drumstick.

"How's your sin chicken?" Karla asked.

"So good!" Vivian closed her eyes and licked her lips. "You want some?"

"No thanks," Karla replied. "If you only get to eat it twice a year, you should savor every bite. So, besides for your legal gymnastics, what do you do to unwind from your work?"

"Lately, I've become obsessed with a series of mystery novels from the 1960s about a rabbi who uses Talmudic logic to solve murders. The author was clearly using the genre to rant about how assimilated the American Jewish community was becoming at the time."

Karla laughed. "That actually just sounds like work."

"Fair point. I'll consider finding some new hobbies. Any suggestions? From our few encounters, it sounds like you may need to de-stress more than me."

"I take a boxing class," Karla said, gulping her beer. "It feels so good to hit something. Sometimes, I imagine I'm sparring with one of the newspapers or with one of the other campaigns after they take a shot at us. It really takes a load off. You should try it sometime."

That's a sexy image, Vivian thought. "It sounds like there's some work in *your* non-work hobby, too," she said.

They continued to talk: about the different voting blocs that Karla and Mike were obsessing over; about what messes, left by DeSoto's untimely death, the new mayor would have to clean up. Before they knew it, it was eleven and the bar was closing.

As they rose and started toward the door, they were still deep in conversation. Not wanting it to end, Vivian offered Karla a ride home.

"I only live a few blocks from here," Karla said, "but you can walk with me if you want."

Vivian agreed. She had been so focused on their conversation that she'd forgotten this particular juncture was key to deciphering whether or not it had been a date. *It feels like a date,* she thought, *but is it normal to discuss the ins and outs of tax relief for housing development on a date? A really good date?*

"Charter schools are moving in whether we like it or not," Karla continued, as they walked at identical paces down an empty block of closed storefronts. "Our goal is to work with them to create better support structures for both students and teachers. My ex-boyfriend taught for a few years at a charter school, and he burnt out so quickly. If this is what will work economically for the city, we have to figure out a way to embrace it while making sure it also works for the students and for the faculty."

Vivian wanted to challenge Karla on the position of just accepting charter schools as the fate of the education system (a position she, in turn, had picked up from her crush in New York), but all she could think about was the mention of an ex-boyfriend. Was it possible that she had read all the signals wrong? Was Karla straight? Bisexual? A lesbian with an ex-boy-friend? Was she purposely hinting that she was not interested?

Everything was going so well. The signs were all there. And now the confusion, the ambiguity, the self-doubt, all came flooding back. In fact, Vivian realized that she had never made it clear that she herself was gay.

On a quiet street of renovated brownstones, Karla abruptly brought her exposition on education to a close. "Well, this is me."

They stood there, looking at each other. Vivian was not sure, but she thought that Karla stepped toward her. It was late, and Vivian's confusion and exhaustion from a long day overtook her excitement. In the stillness, she could feel Karla's confusion too. Neither of them wanted to leave.

"So, Vivian, um, was this a date?" Karla asked, putting her hands in her pants pockets, breaking the silence. This was the time to cut through the ambiguity, the kind Vivian had experienced several times before, when two women speak for hours and have what starts to seem like chemistry, and yet none of it is spoken aloud.

Vivian had decided on the way to the bar that she would be bold. "If you want it to have been a date, then yes." She clenched her fists, trying not to lose it. "It was a date."

"Then...I enjoyed our date."

Standing in front of Karla's purple door, on the quiet street, on this beautiful spring evening, Vivian wanted to kiss her. She found Karla's confidence contagious. It made her nervous and self-assured all at once. Her heart was beating fast.

"I kind of want to kiss you," she said.

"You don't sound totally sure."

Heather's voice was in Vivian's head. What *would* Ruth Bader Ginsburg do?

"I definitely want to kiss you," Vivian said, taking a step forward. Then she froze. Karla filled in the space, hunching down a little to Vivian's height, and pressed her lips gently against Vivian's.

Vivian pulled away and looked into Karla's green eyes. Her fingers drifted toward Karla's torso. She leaned in to kiss her again, this time with a little more force. Their bodies moved closer together.

"Never thought I'd kiss a rabbi," Karla said, opening her eyes.

"And?" Vivian said, holding a steady gaze.

"I guess I've been missing out."

When they walked away from each other, Karla into her house, Vivian back toward her car, Vivian felt her whole body throb. She wanted more than that kiss. But she could wait. As she drove home, speeding the whole way while pop radio blasted old Taylor Swift, she was calmed by the newfound certainty. She and Karla had had A Date.

FIFTEEN

RAYMOND FIDGETED ALL DAY. With the mop. With his tools. With the mail. Despite the many times that Joseph, or Harry, or those that came before them had said, "Whatever you need, Raymond!"—raises, days off when Mac was sick, or when he was sick—he still rationed his asks.

When Mac was younger, Raymond had coached his middle school baseball team. Raymond loved it. Mac loved it, most of the time. The rest of the boys had been fond of Raymond: how, while they were in the batter's box, he would make funny faces from the third-base line to calm them down; how now and then he would give out game balls not for the most hits, but for hustle, or a good, messy slide into home plate, or offering to throw with one of the mediocre players during warm-ups.

In Raymond's second year of coaching, his responsibilities at Beth Abraham had increased, along with his paycheck. He had become the on-call handyman, and had often stayed late to lock up. Balancing it all became too difficult. So he found another parent to take over coaching the following year. Mac still brought it up when he was angry at Raymond, and so many years later, those jabs still hit him like a wild pitch to the arm.

Around lunchtime, Raymond walked toward Joseph's office, since he had gathered from extensive research trials that Joseph was always more jovial when he was eating. He knocked on the open door.

"Good afternoon, Rabbi."

"Raymond!" Joseph said, wiping his mouth with a napkin. "What can I do for you?"

Raymond walked in, not knowing if he should sit down or remain standing. He stopped somewhere in between the door and the chairs set out for visitors.

"Rabbi, you know my son, Mac?"

"Of course!" Joseph said, smiling. "You used to bring him here all the time. He must be getting toward the end of high school by my calculations. Where will he.... How is he doing these days?"

Raymond knew what question Joseph hesitated to ask. *Where will he be going to college?* He had heard Joseph ask this of congregants countless times.

Raymond's hands were shaking. He clasped them together so Joseph would not notice. "He's good. Working and taking classes at Providence Community College." He tried not to get stuck there, in the chasm between his life and Rabbi Joseph Glass's life and the lives of the families of Beth Abraham.

"A few days ago, he was roughed up by a police officer for no good reason," Raymond said, willing himself to keep going despite his firm belief that this was a pointless exercise. "He and his friends and a lot of other people think we should give less money to the police and more to uh, schools and afford-able housing and stuff like that. And they're trying to find some more, uh, diverse supporters." He hesitated again. Joseph picked at his Tupperware, even though it was empty.

"Mac was hoping," Raymond continued, "and I was hop-ing, that you could sign a letter to the city council about all that and...." Raymond trailed off, not knowing all the ins and outs of the ask. Or perhaps just trapped by the futility of his own efforts.

"I'm so sorry to hear that, Raymond. What happened? What did he...what happened?"

Again, Raymond knew what Joseph had been starting to ask. *What did he do?*

"Nothing," Raymond said. "He rode his bike past a red light and got thrown against a police car."

"I'm sorry to hear that," Joseph said.

Again with the apologies, Raymond thought. Joseph had a reputation for being a skilled pastoral rabbi who knew how to sit with people, who knew how to fill up the right amount of space. Raymond had watched him over the years as he con-soled families in the synagogue after the death of a loved one, through a sickness or a divorce. At first, Joseph used to promise too much. "It will be okay," he would say, reflexively. But after Joseph had had, apparently, enough experiences of things not turning out okay, Raymond had noticed that he spoke less and nodded more.

"Let me talk it over with some people on the board," Joseph said.

They take years to make decisions. I'm asking you, Rabbi, Raymond wanted to say. Instead he bowed his head, accepting the plan, and turned toward the open door.

SIXTEEN

A FTER SWIFT APPROVAL of the minutes, Harry moved the board on to new business. "We've got a packed agenda, so let's get started."

In a bland, windowless multi-purpose room of Beth Abraham, nine out of the board's thirteen members conducted the ritual of their monthly meeting.

"First up, the budget," Harry said. "Our membership numbers are lower again this year. We gained seven new families with young children but lost sixteen households in the meantime."

"What's the breakdown of the sixteen?" Joel Fishman asked.

"Eight empty-nesters who discontinued, three who moved, and five older widows and widowers who passed away. If this trend continues, our bottom line will take a big hit. Now, along-side declining membership, we need to consider rising property taxes, our plans for renovation, and increased security costs. At this rate, we will have an average annual shortfall of $120,000." Harry felt he was in tip-top CEO form.

"It's good to hear that at least our experimentation with new programs is steadily attracting young families," Vera said.

Harry folded his arms, eying the cheese plate and dough-nuts in the middle of the table. Today was the day he had signed up to fast in order to counteract any misfortune potentially caused by the dropping of the Torah several weeks back. There were still a few minutes before his fast ended.

His attention shifted back to Vera. "That won't cut it, Vera. Membership is $2,500 a year. Even if we doubled the numbers of new member households we attract annually and threw in some extra Hebrew school tuitions and donations, we would only gain about $60,000 per year. We need revenue." Harry folded his hands and planted them on the table. "It's time to move on our vacant plot."

Joel Fishman looked up from the printed agenda he was doodling on, excited. "Maybe now the time is ripe for the Jew-ish senior housing community that we've talked about!"

"Joel, my man," Harry said, "we have been holding onto this piece of land for years without moving on it. There have been some proposals over time, but we haven't budged. While it's a nice idea to create a community for some of our seniors, Will Gould has made us a very generous and very real offer." Harry paused for effect. "1.5 million."

Heads snapped up around the long table.

"1.5 million? That would put us in the black for years!" Phil Katz said.

"For condos, right? That's what Will builds?" Vera asked, her voice deeper than usual.

"That's right," said Harry.

"What if we put together a proposal for the board for the senior project?" asked Joel, wiping his forehead.

"You've been saying you would do that for years," said Phil, swatting the air dismissively.

"But now we have the motivation."

Harry intervened. "Come on, everyone, it's clear that Will's offer is the best we are going to get. And then we can be done with it. We don't have to do any more work." Harry looked straight at Joel, who was snacking on a doughnut. "Just to play this out, Joel, if we were to explore the senior community option, are you going to put together a budget, interview contractors, work with Medicare?"

"We could put together a new committee—"

"Joel, a committee will not get this done. Let's see the land for what it is. A chance to get in the black and have a cushion. We can figure out other ways to support our seniors. Maybe we'll add a second bagel brunch each week or something."

Other board members nodded around the table as Vera snorted and focused on a spot outside the window. Harry turned to Joseph. "Rabbi, what do you think?"

Joseph sighed. "I think it's in the best interest of our community to take Will's deal."

"What if you just give us until the next board meeting to put a plan together?" Joel asked.

"Sure, Joel," Harry said. "Put a committee together, talk to the powers that be, and get us a proposal by next month."

Harry slapped the table for closure. "Onto the next order of business. The spring fundraiser!" He looked at his watch. His fast was over. He grabbed a doughnut from the plate at the center of the table and took a satisfied bite.

. . .

Joseph and Harry lingered after the meeting, discussing next steps on Will's proposal. As the conversation wound down, Joseph saw an opening and raised Raymond's request with Harry.

"What did his kid do?" Harry said, still nibbling on leftover refreshments.

"Raymond says nothing. I trust him."

"How can we be sure?" Harry said, walking toward the entrance. "We don't know the kid. I mean, sure, maybe when he was six or seven, but who knows what he's like now. Rabbi, come on. You know better than anyone how much effort we've put into building a good relationship with Chief Thicke, with the rest of the force. We have to hold on to that."

Joseph cupped his beard and nodded, fighting back his desire to say more, to make a better case for adding his name to a measly letter. But he too understood that the battle they had chosen, that he had chosen, was to secure Will Gould's money. There was only so much capital to spend.

SEVENTEEN

WHILE THE TENSE MEETING dragged on at Beth Abraham, Vivian found herself at a dance studio across town. Historically, she loved to dance. With friends, girlfriends, maybe-girlfriends. Dancing had once given her the space to step into queerness. She learned how her body could move with a feminine grace and a touch of masculine edge all at once. She learned to sense the magnetic pull of attraction between her and a woman from across the room who followed Vivian with her eyes. She learned she wanted that.

After she was ordained, she had had trouble squaring her identity as a rabbi with this routine. Vivian had worked hard to shake old images of what people—what she—thought a rabbi should look like. But she could not let go of one preposterous vision: three bearded old men staring her down with disdainful eyes in a night club. It was soon after her ordination that the panel of rabbis first appeared to her at her favorite dance spot in Brooklyn, sitting on bar stools, drinking wine from their kiddush cups and shaking their heads in disapproval.

Zumba class, however, felt safe from the judgment. Lisa's partner, Bree, who'd lived most of her life in the South Side neighborhood that was home to this dance studio, had invited Vivian along. She was loving the hip-hop moves, the top-forty hits with catchy beats. It was exactly what she needed. She spent so much of the day in her head (and sometimes in her heart), she often forgot she had a body, a body that could move, that could feel better when she let it be free, creative.

Music blasted through the room and Vivian mirrored the instructor's steps. With each song, her body loosened further, as though every move dislodged something rigid and stuck inside her. Her only hiccups were the salsa moves. Something about the particular foot coordination they required always tripped her up, so she ran in place instead. Dancing beside Vivian, Bree giggled when she noticed this strategy.

After the class cooled down to a Beyoncé ballad, Vivian and Bree, sweaty and out of breath, made their way to the water fountain to fill up their bottles.

"Wow, I needed that. Thanks, Bree."

"You should come back," Bree said, wiping her face with the bottom of her t-shirt. "Maybe even for a salsa lesson," she added, arching an eyebrow in challenge.

As they hydrated and caught their breath on one of the

benches lining the studio, Vivian switched topics. "I heard that one of your big work projects fell through. I'm sorry to hear that."

"That's how it goes," Bree said, packing her sneakers into her gym bag. "These developers, they put on fancy suits and drink high-end liquor, wheeling and dealing, but they are really just children. Bullies, building with their Legos and toppling over the others." She slipped on her flip-flops. "We had plans practically set for a mixed-income development that would have created pathways for Black homeownership. Then we faltered for one moment when some public funding was pulled, and before we could re-secure it, Barry Brook snuck around and grabbed the land right out from under us."

Vivian zipped up her sweatshirt. "I wish my synagogue could just sell you our vacant parcel."

"The Banks Street lot? I think we looked into it a few years ago, when it was clear that there weren't too many options in our catchment area, but we didn't get anywhere. From what my boss told me, the leadership was tough to work with." Bree covered her mouth. "Oh, sorry if that's offensive."

"I'm well aware," Vivian said, halfheartedly practicing a dance move she was hoping to commit to memory.

"What's the plan for that property?" Bree asked.

"We are probably going to sell it to Riverside Developers and it will become just another set of luxury condos," Vivian said. Joseph had shared the developments with Vivian earlier in the week, speaking slowly as he described the nighttime phone call from Will, as though he was admitting a wrongdoing. "Will Gould, the CEO, is a member of our congregation, and everyone fawns over him. They're probably pushing the plan forward as we speak, at the board meeting I'm not invited to tonight."

"You know, it's not that different," Bree said, shaking her head, "Brook stealing land right out from under us, and Gould getting his friends to do his bidding. The powerful do what they will and the rest of us have to live with it."

Perhaps it was the endorphins, or the hovering presence of the sage Beyoncé, but Vivian was ready for a fight, to take a risk. "Seems like a long shot, but let me see if I can plant some seeds. Some people on the board have wanted the property to be used for a retirement community, but haven't been willing to put in the work. If they were handed a project that was already set, and the senior piece could be added in, maybe everyone could win?"

Bree laughed. "Everyone except All-Powerful Will Gould."

Vivian slapped at the air as if that complication were a small fly, easily dismissed. They walked out of the studio and into the night. "Will can certainly move fast," Vivian said. "But getting our board to come to agreement in just one meeting, I don't think even *he* could pull that off."

"I'm not going to hold my breath," Bree said. "But I appreciate your creativity. Let me know how it goes. Depending on who wins the mayor's race there might be more public money on the table for a project like that." They parted ways, each walking back toward their cars.

"Hey," Bree called back over her shoulder, "Have you ever considered joining our side? You seem to have a knack for it."

EIGHTEEN

A S HARRY WAS putting on his plaid pajamas after returning home from the board meeting, his cell phone rang.

"Hiya, Harry!"

"Hi, Will," Harry said, replacing the Bluetooth earpiece that he had just removed. "How's the Caribbean?" Will was calling from a family vacation.

"Beautiful," Will said. "Just what I needed! Obviously, I'm still working most of the day, but at least it's in the sun with a margarita, you know? So, how'd the meeting go? Do we have a deal?"

"Not quite, but we are getting there," Harry said.

"What do you mean, 'We are getting there?' How could anyone turn down one and a half million just for that land?"

"Will, we'll make the deal soon," Harry said, trying to make sense of Will's tone. "We just have to play this out. You know how these—"

"Harry, you were supposed to be my closer," Will said. "How could you have dropped the ball on this?"

Harry was perplexed. He and Will were friends, they ran the show together. Harry from the front, Will from the back. "Calm down, Will. We'll take a vote at the next board meeting, the one after that at the latest. What's the rush?"

"Harry, we had a plan, and you screwed it up."

"We'll get this done. I promise," Harry tried to reassure him.

"I don't have time for—just get it done, okay?" Will hung up without giving Harry a moment to respond.

NINETEEN

THE NEXT MORNING, a weary Joseph hid in his office, avoiding Raymond. As he put the finishing touches on his sermon for the next night, Joseph could not stop thinking about Raymond, about Mac; about how when Mac was little, he had spent many quiet summer days at the synagogue.

Whenever Joseph's teenaged son, Jake, stopped by, Mac would somehow convince him to play hide-and-seek. Mac would hide all over the building, constantly finding new spots where Jake did not think to look.

One time, he tiptoed into Joseph's office, without saying a word, and squeezed himself into a tiny space between a bookshelf and the wall. When Jake came looking, Joseph could see six-year-old Mac out of the corner of his eye, giggling silently, covering his mouth with his finger. An appeal for loyalty. "I haven't seen him, Jake," Joseph had told his son. After Jake left to continue the search, Mac had run over to Joseph and raised his hand for a high five. Joseph reciprocated and Mac immediately dashed out the door, laughing the whole time.

Joseph kept looking over to that same nook where Mac had been hiding, imagining him in it now, making his convincing plea. Joseph could not avoid Raymond all day. He needed a book from the library, too, and he finally left his office to retrieve it. On the way, he ran into Raymond, who was repainting a patch of the wall where a Hebrew school student had scribbled in permanent marker.

"Good afternoon, Rabbi," Raymond said.

"Hey, Raymond," Joseph said, stopping to face him. "Listen, I brought up your question, you know, about signing that letter, with some folks on the board. I think, for now, it seems like this isn't the kind of thing we can do as a synagogue. Or that I can do as the rabbi. There isn't a precedent for it or anything." Joseph looked down at his hands, folding them in and out of each other. "But let me know if we can support you and Mac in any other way."

Raymond nodded, expressionless. To Joseph, it seemed that he was not surprised, but that it still hurt. Being on the outside, even after being inside the building for so long, probably never stopped hurting, Joseph thought.

TWENTY

VIVIAN GUESSED FIFTY-THREE people in the sanctuary from her big red chair on the bima. She had become skilled in the jellybean-jar-style guessing game that Joseph taught her. As the congregation chanted one of the psalms of Kabbalat Shabbat along with Joseph, two young, unfamiliar faces entered the room. Fifty-five.

From afar, they seemed to Vivian like a couple. A young man in a blazer and jeans put his hand gently on the woman's back, catching her curls, over a bright, flower-patterned sundress. The man was White and the woman was Black. After taking prayer books from the greeter, they hesitantly took seats toward the back. Vivian had never seen them before. Her mind tried to compute this strange occurrence: two people who looked to be in their late twenties, one a woman of color, voluntarily entering services with no parents in sight. Vivian wondered if the timing coincided with some university break, but she could not think of any in early May.

She wondered whether to go greet them but decided that it was more important to stay rooted in her prayers. Not many congregants expressed theirs physically. Most just stood and sat still while the leader and some percentage of the congregation sang together. Vivian often found that demonstrably feeling her prayers, and not being embarrassed about it, created room for others to do the same. She remained in her seat, rocking her shoulders back and forth, feigning devotion.

In the middle of *Lecha Dodi*, the prayer that welcomes Shabbat as though she were a bride, Vivian noticed the young couple scrunching their faces and shifting in their seats. They whispered to one another, then glanced at Vivian. The woman rose and took a few steps toward the entrance. She stood for a moment, looking out, then swiftly returned to her seat and whispered to the man. They both looked at Vivian, this time with wider eyes.

Vivian was steadfast in her decision not to smother them. *If I go over there, I might say the wrong thing. Or they'll think I'm desperate, hovering.*

But their looks kept coming. Around the sixth verse, hoping no one would notice, Vivian stood up from her chair and walked toward them. She ran her finger along the wood-paneled wall and over the crevices of the golden Tree of Life whose leaves bore the names of deceased congregants. She wondered what greeting would strike the right tone, how not to say something that would make the woman feel out of place.

"Shabbat shalom!" she whispered, kneeling down when she reached them. "I'm Rabbi Vivian. It's so nice to have you with us tonight. Do you need anything? Can I help you find the page?" she offered. Vivian hoped her calm and nonchalant approach would preclude any interpretations of smothering.

"Um, I didn't want to interrupt, but I think the synagogue is on fire," the woman said.

Vivian furrowed her brow. She wondered whether this woman's comment was literal or metaphorical. The metaphor did not match the expression on her face. But the literal possibility seemed far less likely. Perhaps it was some commentary on Beth Abraham's severely off-putting racial dynamic. Vivian considered how to respond. After all, it was exciting to have new young energy at the service, and she wanted so much for them to have a good experience, and—

She finally smelled the smoke. Vivian scanned the room, sniffing audibly. Focusing on the small glass windows in the sanctuary doors, she spotted their shifting shapes. "Oh, you mean the synagogue is *actually* on fire."

"Right, that's what I said," the woman whispered loudly.

Vivian spent a split second trying to interpret her response. What was this couple's impression of the community? Of her? Had she said the wrong thing? To Vivian, it felt as though the prospect of someday attracting younger people and more Jews of Color to Beth Abraham rested on the shoulders of this bizarre interaction in this bizarre moment.

Then it hit her. Beth Abraham was on fire! She ran toward

the back of the sanctuary. Vivian looked toward Joseph, who was leading from the bima, mouthing the prayers in a routine way. She considered if she should consult with him, but there was no time. The group had just risen to their feet for the final verse of *Lecha Dodi* when all turn around in their seats to face the door and welcome Shabbat. As a result, Vivian was now standing directly at the front of the entire congregation.

"I'm so sorry to interrupt such spirited prayer," she shouted, "just as we welcome the Shabbat bride, but it seems as though the building is on fire." Cutting off the congregation just at this moment when they were finally praying with their bodies, willing the energy of Shabbat to enter the room, seemed almost sinful to Vivian. It felt as though she had just shattered a glass. A few voices continued to sing, speak, question, like broken shards no longer part of a whole vessel. But the disparate sounds quickly dissipated and gave way to a strange, incomplete silence, wholly unlike the silence following a communal prayer that had reached its expected end. Vivian looked forward for affirmation, for backup. But from her vantage point in the back of the room, Joseph looked small and powerless.

"Again, I am so sorry, but the synagogue is on fire. There is an emergency exit through the classroom right outside the sanctuary," Vivian shouted, waving her hand behind her, pointing toward the door. As the voices around her started to get louder, she looked around to see who she could enlist for assistance. She spotted Vera.

"Vera, will you lead the group to the exit?" Vera seemed caught off-guard. But after placing her siddur on her chair, and then changing her mind and picking it back up, she took the assignment in stride. She waved her hand in the air and marched with purpose toward the hallway door through the crowd and through the shrieks.

Some of the regulars followed first, which gave permission to the less-than-regulars, including the newcomers Vivian had been so preoccupied with, to join in what looked like a frantic conga line toward the door. The smoke was gaining on them, and once they entered the hallway, congregants began to cough and choke. Vivian noticed Joseph slowly shepherding the group from the rear, with Gert Fineman, one of Beth Abraham's oldest members, on his arm. Moving through the thickening cloud toward the emergency exit, the line of people reached the Hebrew school classroom and hurried through the door to the outside.

Vivian remained inside until everyone had safely exited. She thought of all the holy objects in the shul and was reminded of the question posed to her when she had created her defunct online dating profile: *What is the one thing you would take with you in a fire?* She had written her grandmother's candlesticks, even though the real answer was the four-hundred-dollar pair of leather boots that she bought when she signed her contract, which made her look like her hottest gay self. But in the case of the synagogue, she thought of the Torah scrolls right away, and knew she could not rescue all four. Covering her mouth with her tallit, she ran up to the front of the sanctuary, opened the ark and took one out: the one that had been dropped weeks before, the one with the broken spindle.

"Rabbi Vivian, come on, you've got to get out!" someone shouted from a distance. It was Raymond. "I've done a sweep of the building, I think it's clear."

"Raymond, would you feel comfortable, I mean…." Vivian stumbled on her question as she yelled back. "Could you—would you—take one of these Torahs?" It was not the time to hesitate, look for the right words, but she knew it was a strange request. It was not as though Raymond had the same responsibility to the scrolls.

He looked behind him, the smoke curling closer and closer. He ran up to the ark and awkwardly tried to grip one of the scrolls inside. "How do you hold this thing?" Raymond asked.

"Here, take this." Vivian handed him the one that she was holding. She took one of the other three out of the ark, just as though it was Shabbat morning and she was about to lead a procession around the room in which all the congregants would kiss the scroll, absorb some of its holiness.

Vivian and Raymond rushed toward the door, holding fast to the sacred objects. Coughing up smoke as the flames rounded the hallway, reaching toward them, they ducked into the classroom and out of the emergency exit.

TWENTY-ONE

MORE FIREFIGHTERS THAN Vivian could count had surrounded the building to extinguish the flames, but not before much of the interior of the synagogue was destroyed. Some congregants talked, some cried and embraced one another, and others left. There was no ritual for something like this, for the direct aftermath. There was just shock. And ash.

Vivian could see Gert Fineman in the distance, sitting in her old black Buick, being comforted by several others whom Vivian could only glimpse through all the commotion. Looking back toward the flames, she noticed Raymond leading some of the firefighters to the side of the building where the kitchen was.

After setting down the Torah on a table half-covered in

medical supplies, Vivian found the young couple standing at the edge of the cluster of Beth Abraham members that had formed in the parking lot.

"Are you all right?" Vivian said. "I promise, it's not always like this."

"We're okay. And it seems like everyone got out," the woman said.

"A bunch of people have been checking in on us," the man said. "Very graciously," he added. Vivian's gaze remained on the woman, trying to discern if she, too, would characterize the greetings as gracious. She bristled at the thought of her congregants trying to make a good impression, fumbling to say the right things.

"Come back whenever you want." As they both nodded tentatively, Vivian realized the ridiculousness of her parting words. Did they really need an invitation? Would there even be a shul to come back to? But she wanted so much for them to return.

"Another time, Rabbi Vivian," the man said.

Vivian still stood there, not wanting to leave. "What are your names?"

"I'm Flora, and this is Ben," the woman said.

Vivian noticed commotion around the ambulances. But before leaving Flora and Ben, she craved a closure, something close to normalcy. So she reached her hand out to shake each of theirs. "Nice to meet you," Vivian said. They both shook weakly.

Vivian moved on, making her way toward the ambulance parked nearby. Tamar Benayoun was sitting in the back of it, coughing nonstop. "It's protocol to take you in for smoke inhalation," one of the medics said.

"Can't I just wait for my husband?" Tamar pleaded. "He's working, but he'll be off in a few hours. I need him with me."

Vivian examined the crowd. Cars were lined up at the exit. Many community members were making their way home, and the fire department was on the case. She climbed up the back of the van and sat with Tamar. "I'll go with you, Tamar. We can call Perry on the way."

"But Rabbi," Tamar spoke through her coughs, "you don't drive on Shabbat."

"Your wellbeing is more important."

As the ambulance left, and the sirens started to sound again, Tamar cried between her coughs. Vivian reached out and took her hand. They said nothing. Vivian began to hum a tune to one of the psalms from Kabbalat Shabbat. "Always keep a niggun in your pocket," a teacher of hers once said. At first, Vivian had to work to remember, to find the right tune. But over time, the melodies easily became a language Vivian could speak, in which each song communicated just what was needed.

Vivian and Tamar spent that Shabbat evening in the hospital. After a few hours of waiting and reading trashy magazines they found on the side tables, a doctor called for Tamar. A nurse offered her some oxygen to calm her cough. Tamar's husband, who had been working late at a different hospital across town, arrived to take her home just as she was cleared to go.

Vivian had only been in a car a handful of times on Shabbat. She was strict about her practice but learned to make exceptions in the face of other priorities: her best friend's wedding, a few other trips to the hospital to be with family or friends. Though it seemed to qualify as a legitimate reason to break

Shabbat, she turned down Perry's offer for a ride. She wanted to be alone in the quiet spring night and walk the two miles home.

She strolled past the homes, the closed storefronts on Main Street. It was well past midnight and Providence was quiet. She thought about the smoke. She thought about the flames burning through the kitchen, the classrooms, the sanctuary. She thought about Flora, second-guessing everything she had said to her. She thought about the Torahs she could not save, the books, the beautiful art on the drab walls.

Vivian was struck with an image of the burning bush, of Moses noticing the spectacle because the fire did not consume it. Because it was holy, because the fire was God's presence. She remembered the midrash in which Abraham was thrown into the fire as a child but not consumed. *But fire always consumes, injures, maims*, she protested in her mind.

As Main Street faded into residential streets, she realized that she was in Karla's neighborhood. Vivian was suddenly so exhausted, so in need of being wrapped in someone's embrace. Without her phone, she had no way of getting in touch with Karla, and though she was dimly aware that it was socially unacceptable, she felt an urge to go knock on her door.

She walked the streets she remembered from their date and up to Karla's purple front door. She stood there, still, humming to herself. She knocked softly. No answer. She knocked again with more force. A light flickered on in the front window. A sleepy Karla opened the door.

Karla blinked several times to register what she was seeing. Vivian was standing in front of her, with traces of soot on her face and teary eyes.

"There was a fire at the synagogue tonight during services," Vivian said.

Karla yawned widely and then suddenly processed what she had heard. "Are you okay? Is everyone okay?"

"No one was seriously injured." Vivian paused. "I...I don't want to be alone tonight."

Karla offered a sleepy smile. "Come in," she said.

Vivian followed her through the entrance. The apartment was sleek. Vivian noticed one of the better-quality Ikea couches. It was a bold blue with nicely complementary yellow pillows. There were books everywhere, glowing wood floors and new appliances in the kitchen. Vivian had already been imagining Karla's apartment, and kissing her on a medium-quality Ikea couch.

In silence, Karla rummaged through the middle drawer of her dresser before settling on striped pajama pants and a Wesleyan Crew t-shirt. She folded them neatly onto the unmade bed from which she had clearly just been disturbed.

Vivian stared at the pajamas. "I'm sorry to put you out like this." They stood at a distance from each other, still. "Is this weird? Me being here?"

"It sounds like it's been a weird night all around," Karla said. "And I'm glad you're here." Karla drew in closer and took Vivian's hand, slipping her fingers through Vivian's. "I don't have an extra toothbrush," she continued, "but you can use mine."

Vivian, feeling confused about what boundaries did and did not exist between the two of them, took the pajamas from the bed into the bathroom. There, she looked at her face in the mirror, at the streaks of ash that remained. Her eyes looked tired, her clothes wrinkled. She sniffed them. Smoke. Silently, a few tears rolled down her cheek.

Under the showerhead, she washed herself, gently at first and then with more vigor, in order to cleanse her body of all the soot and grief. She stepped out of the shower and dried off, wondering if the towel that she had grabbed had recently been wrapped around Karla. She then put on the pajamas. Looking in the mirror again, she thought about all the other circumstances that could have brought her to this point, to Karla's bed.

Hesitantly, she squeezed toothpaste onto Karla's toothbrush. She brushed her teeth quickly, trying not to think about how much she disliked using other people's toothbrushes. As she put her hand on the bathroom doorknob, she did not know what would happen. This all felt too intimate too quickly. And yet, on this strange night, it was what she needed.

Vivian turned the knob and walked back to Karla's bed. She was sitting up, reading *The New Yorker* by the light of a small lamp.

"Ah, some light middle-of-the-night reading." Vivian said. "Anything good?"

"Just an essay about survivalists in Silicon Valley, hoarding resources in preparation for the apocalypse," Karla said, tearing her eyes from the page and then looking at Vivian with exaggerated panic.

"Well, perhaps we've both had some intensity tonight then."

"You know, this is freaking me out," Karla said. "I'm glad you're here to keep me company."

Vivian laughed. A few more tears ran down her cheeks. She wiped them away. She hesitantly lifted the duvet cover and climbed into bed. Karla put the magazine down on her nightstand and sank into the cotton sheets. They were facing each other. "Will you just hold me?" Vivian whispered.

Karla nodded. Vivian turned around and curled up her body. Karla drew closer and fit her body to Vivian's, putting her arms around Vivian's waist and gently kissing the back of her head. Vivian closed her wet eyes and fell asleep.

TWENTY-TWO

WHEN VIVIAN AWOKE the next morning to the sun shining through a foreign window, she could not place where she was. Only an imprint of Karla's body remained next to her. Memories of the night before flooded back. Reluctant to face the day and Karla, Vivian buried her head in the pillow. *Well, that's one way to get in her bed*, she thought.

She could hear Karla moving around in the kitchen. Something was sizzling and she smelled coffee. She stretched her arms toward the ceiling, willing the rest of her body to stand upright.

"Good morning. How are you feeling?" Karla asked, without turning around, as Vivian approached.

"I've been better," Vivian replied. She sat down at the island that separated the kitchen and living room and continued, "I had a nightmare about Silicon Valley survivalists waging war on the rest of us. So now I'm just recovering." Karla chuckled.

"I think I'm okay," Vivian went on. "My body's fine. No one got hurt. But what do I do now? What do you do the morning after you escape a fire?"

"Call your family?" Karla said.

"They won't pick up on Shabbat," she said, wiping the sleep from her eyes.

"Right," Karla said. "Then I guess you eat some breakfast."

Karla poured coffee, scooped eggs and toast onto a plate, and set both down on the counter in front of Vivian. Then she made herself a serving and settled onto the stool next to hers.

"Thank you." Vivian said.

"You're welcome. This is certainly a memorable second date." Their eyes locked.

"What's on your docket today?" Vivian said, looking away.

"We have some breakfasts with different community groups that I've got to get to in about an hour. Both in senior housing buildings. Those are usually easy gigs. They just talk a lot and ask questions about transportation. Speaking of which, do you need a ride anywhere? Back to the synagogue?"

"I think I'll walk there and see what's going on," Vivian said, trying and failing to skewer some eggs onto her fork. "I'm sure everyone is already freaking out that…." She lifted the fork and a nearly invisible amount of egg into her mouth, leaving her thought unfinished.

"Are you sure?" Karla asked. "I could drop you off a few blocks away, so they'd never know."

"Thanks, but it's not too far, and I could use the air," Vivian said, finally managing to procure a sizeable bite. "Plus, I can't have you thinking I have no integrity in my observance of Jewish law."

"Ah, yes, the sin chicken," Karla said, leaning back in her chair. "At least now I have a diverse picture of what a rabbi can be."

Vivian's eyes crinkled. She dabbed her mouth with a napkin. "But there is one thing I need. My clothes smell like smoke. Could I borrow some of yours?"

"I bet we can find something," Karla said, seeming to consider the five-inch height difference between them. "I've got a few pantsuits you could choose from. You could pin up the bottoms."

"Got any skirts?" Vivian said. "That's more my style."

Karla piled up the dishes and dropped them in the sink. "I think there are a few in the back of my closet that I save for occasions that never seem to come up." She disappeared into her bedroom and Vivian followed.

Karla pulled a navy pencil skirt and a light blue button-down shirt out of the closet. "These should work."

"This shirt fits quite well," Vivian said as she tried it on, in the corner of the room, turned away from Karla. Vivian finished putting on the clothes and looked in the closet mirror. "Wow, no one would ever know I unexpectedly spent the night somewhere."

"Perks of being a homo, I guess," Karla said.

As they stood in the doorway minutes later, prepared for their days, Vivian leaned over and kissed her. She kissed back and wrapped her arms around Vivian's shoulders. Vivian's hand drifted up to Karla's cheek. Karla pulled back and looked into her eyes. Vivian kissed her one more time, a soft peck.

"Shabbat shalom," Karla said.

"Shabbat shalom."

Karla walked to her car, and Vivian started down the block, into the quiet glow of Saturday morning.

TWENTY-THREE

VIVIAN ARRIVED AT Beth Abraham not knowing what to expect—not knowing if there was cleanup work to do, even on Shabbat, or if the Saturday-morning regulars would show up oblivious to the events of the previous night.

The damage was more visible in the morning light. As the building came into focus when Vivian neared it, the reality of the fire set in. The sanctuary's beautiful stained-glass windows were chipped and darkened. The left side of the synagogue, where most of the Hebrew school classrooms and the kitchen were situated, had turned various gradations of gray and black. The grass and flowers that lined the walkway along the exterior were trampled and colorless. Vivian's whole body stiffened.

A fire truck and two police vehicles were parked in the lot, alongside just a few cars. The regulars had, in fact, gotten the message. Vivian later learned that Harry had spent most of the night emailing and calling people to let them know what happened. He didn't ask Joseph what was and was not appropriate to do on Shabbat in this instance. Making the calls to this group, those Harry knew would pick up on a Friday night, seemed a more rational move than allowing for a repeat occurrence of surprise and shock. They were all too depleted for that.

Vivian noticed that the kitchen door was open, and saw a police officer walk in. She followed him inside. The space was unrecognizable, wet and black with debris scattered all around. A few firefighters were lifting severed appliance parts, others were bending down to examine the discoloration. Joseph, Harry, Raymond, and Phil Katz—who had headed the committee that oversaw renovations some years back—stood silently in the back corner, watching, wearing plastic facemasks to avoid inhaling dangerous chemicals. Vivian remained still in the entrance amid the noisy silence.

She thought of the Torah portion that they were supposed to have read in shul that morning, had they been following the regularly scheduled Shabbat program. It included the blessing, and the potential curse, of water, of natural elements. Do good in the eyes of God and the world, and rain and a steady yield will be your reward, the portion said. Disobey, and the same nourishing water will devastate the land and the people as punishment. Vivian had prepared questions for a study session later that day. A few replayed in her thoughts. *Do we believe that humans' sins cause God to act against us? Have you ever felt rewarded for a good deed or punished for a bad one?*

"Seems like the fire started here in the kitchen, boys."

"Ahem." Vivian coughed in protest of Fire Chief Marco Gonzalez's gender assessment. Noticing her presence, a nearby firefighter leaned over and handed her a facemask.

Gonzalez had reassembled the group in the kitchen; hours earlier, they had spread out throughout the charred building, examining the smallest details of the fire's damage and taking notes. They concluded that the flames had followed a clear trajectory, starting in the kitchen in the back of the building, winding through the hallway of classrooms, and then into the sanctuary, straight toward the ark and the remaining two Torah scrolls.

"Here is what we are working with," Gonzalez said. "There are a few possible sources for a fire like this one. Could be a faulty outlet somewhere in the room. Could be an oven. Could be a compromised extension cord, or the boiler. We can rule out the boiler because it's on the unimpacted side of the building. It doesn't seem like there were any extension cords in use at the time, which leaves us with the oven or a faulty outlet."

"It couldn't have been the oven. It's brand-new, just installed on Friday," Harry said.

Hesitantly, Raymond spoke up. "Actually, the company called to postpone the delivery. I wrote a note with the update, but it must have gotten lost in, you know, all of this." He waved his arms around.

"Aha!" Gonzalez responded. "Let's definitely check the wiring on it. A whole wing of a building doesn't get destroyed without something being off."

"We'll get to the bottom of this," added the police chief, Cal Thicke.

Raymond coughed, trying to clear his throat. Looking around, he noticed the rest of the group noticing him. He could not stop coughing and left the kitchen.

While the professionals continued dissecting charred appliances and wires in search of the fire's source, Vivian looked on, unsure how to be of use. She exited the room, compelled to find Raymond.

She spotted him down the office corridor that the fire had never reached, staring blankly ahead.

"Raymond? Are you okay?"

He turned toward her. His eyes were red. He looked away again, seeming indecisive.

"The police sure as hell won't 'get to the bottom' of things in my neighborhood," he finally said, returning his gaze to Vivian. "Mac, my son, got beaten up by a cop last week."

Vivian gasped, raising her hand in front of her mouth. "Raymond, I'm so sorry." She resettled her arm at her side. "Why didn't you say anything?"

"I told Rabbi Joseph last week."

Vivian shook her head, out of premature frustration at Joseph, out of surprise that Raymond was sharing this with her. "I know I won't ever be able to understand what that feels like, for Mac. For you. But whatever you need, let me know. You are an important member of this community." Raymond groaned and looked away again.

Vivian wished she were closer to him. There were so many people she had had to get to know in her first year at Beth

Abraham, so many people to set up meetings with and take out for coffee. Raymond never rose to the top of her list.

"I asked Joseph if he'd sign onto a letter supporting budget cuts for the police department. Mac has gotten very involved in that campaign," Raymond said, straightening up his back. "Joseph checked with some people on the board, whatever that means—maybe Harry and some others—and apparently they said no." Raymond stopped abruptly. "I'm sorry, I didn't mean...." He did not finish his sentence.

A sadness overcame Vivian. It made its way through her body, her torso, her legs. "I wish this place could feel more like home for you," she said putting her hand against the wall to hold herself up.

Raymond looked down at his shoes. "I know you care, but...." Again, the rest of the sentence never came.

"I haven't met Mac," Vivian said, filling the void. "But if you, if he, still wants someone from the synagogue to sign onto that letter, I'll do it. Maybe we could find a time to talk or—"

"Rabbi Vivian," Raymond interrupted, "I don't want to put you out like that. It's fine. It'll be fine."

Vivian looked into his eyes, trying to communicate what she could not put into words, that she was, or wanted to try to be, better than Joseph and Harry. But she was not sure if her offer was real, if she had the strength, the magic, to bypass the same obstacles Joseph was not willing to. So, she did not push further. With nothing left to say, Raymond walked away.

Vivian dragged herself back to the kitchen, unable to shake the discomfort and the distance she had felt between her and Raymond. The cleanup crew was still searching for the source of the fire, trying to make sense of the evidence. "The kitchen is too wet," Fire Chief Gonzalez said. "And there's too much debris to complete a full investigation. We'll have to come back over the next few days and weeks, collect some more evidence and keep slogging along. These kinds of searches, well, they can take a while."

"What can you tell us that you *do* know, Chief?" Harry asked. "Do you think it was an accident? Or...." He stalled, now looking at Joseph, as if unclear which man could answer his unfinished question.

"It's very possible that it was an accident."

Police Chief Thicke stroked his chin. "Could something have been tampered with? Could this have been done on purpose?"

"We certainly can't rule out arson," Gonzalez said. "Especially since the fire alarm never went off."

TWENTY-FOUR

VERA OPENED HER HOME to all of Beth Abraham the Sunday after the fire. She and her husband, Charlie, were among the handful of people in the congregation who regularly invited guests over for Shabbat meals. They were natural hosts.

This was the first community-wide gathering since the fire. Together, they would pray, grieve, and eat. Joseph and Vivian arrived early to help Charlie and Vera set up the living room. Harry soon arrived with pastries and coffee in hand.

Without a prescribed ritual for transition from destruction to recovery, the rabbis of Beth Abraham looked to the relevant options at their disposal: shiva and lament. These were muscles they knew how to flex.

It happened to be the day Vivian had signed up to fast in the aftermath of the Torah drop. It all felt like a tangled knot to her: the injured scroll, the fire, the scheming about real estate behind closed doors. But now was not the time to make sense of it all. Now was the time to be present, and to help lead her people through this mess.

Members started to trickle in as the afternoon sky softened. By five, around forty members of the congregation had appeared, cramming into Vera's living room. As people moved around the room in a slow rhythm, seeking out friends, Vivian noticed a new-comer walking toward her in a red business suit, a strange outfit for a Sunday. The woman looked very familiar. As she approached, Vivian finally placed her. But what was she doing here?

"Hi, Rabbi," Margaret Heath said, putting out her hand. "It's nice to see you again, though not under the circumstances."

"Yes, thank you for being here. How did you...?" Vivian began to ask as they shook hands.

"I was so sorry to hear about the fire, though I'm glad everyone is okay. I've known Vera for decades, and I ran into her in the supermarket today. Anyway, she let me know about tonight's gathering and invited me to stop by if I wanted to express condolences. I know it must be a difficult and scary time given what's going on these days."

"That's very kind of you," Vivian said, "especially since you probably have a very busy schedule."

"If I can be of any support as you figure out what's next, let me know," Heath said.

"I, um, we will," Vivian said. "Thank you for being here, Ms. Heath."

"Please, Rabbi, call me Margaret." Vivian watched as Margaret Heath made the rounds to some others that she seemed to know before disappearing.

For the first half hour, people schmoozed in the various rooms of Vera and Charlie's spacious first floor. Their house was warm and welcoming. Vivian could hear the ambient sounds of greeting, of grief, of speculation. She had heard some of these voices, in the synagogue during the cleanup, in the calls she split with Joseph to check on older members. And also while alone, lying in bed. *They are after us. Again.* Each time she detected it in her own mind, she willed it away.

Joseph summoned the group to the living room. People began to gather around him. Regulars, not-so-regulars, and several faces that Vivian could barely place took their seats on the furniture and extra folding chairs.

They began with the mincha service led by Sammy Bickel, who remained teary-eyed all through the prayers. As he ended with a special closing psalm, there was a pause, and the eyes of those congregated fell on Joseph. His hands were clasped together over his heart.

"It is good to be together tonight," he began. "Over the past few days, I have been thinking an awful lot about a particular midrash. Before the Israelites built the *mishkan*, the holy tabernacle in the desert, the whole world trembled. It was constantly unsteady. This shaking would only cease if God's power could be contained in one place. And so, the Israelites were instructed to build the mishkan, a permanent container for God's presence, the *shechina*. Once it was built, the trembling ceased. I have always taken this midrash to be a nod to the power of our sacred spaces, our synagogues. We are able to contain what is holy, concentrate it in our beautiful building, and within our community."

Joseph rocked back and forth with folded arms as he spoke. "I know that we all feel this trembling, the unsteadiness, the fear, now that some the power has escaped from our damaged sacred home. But I can assure you all that we will get back to that place. We will rebuild so that we can once again contain the holiness, once again feel the steadiness that provides."

Joseph sat down. He gave no cue as to what should come next in this ritual they were inventing on the spot.

Vivian's voice rose from the quiet. "Perhaps the midrash is not only about the physical space of the mishkan, but also a space that we collectively create together, where we call in God and holiness and steadiness. Like what we are doing here.

"I feel God's contained presence with all of you," Vivian continued, "as our sadness and love and hope and gratitude that no one was more seriously injured fills the room and fills our hearts." The room hummed with a collective sigh. Vivian glanced over at Joseph and he nodded, looking back at her with kind eyes.

. . .

Vivian remained to help clean up after almost everyone had left. A few others did too, including Joel Fishman. While collecting paper plates and coffee cups and reconfiguring the furniture in the living room, Joel wondered aloud what would happen now to the vacant land. "I know now may not be the time," his words came out slowly, "but Joseph's sermon is making me think about our future plans and what we might be able to build anew. I think the senior living community could be just the thing."

After she stacked the folding chairs, Vivian cleared the cheese and cracker plate, surprised that instead of craving a bite after hours of fasting, she was instead overcome by a hunger to create something holy. Perhaps the foreign experience of mourning, of praying, of feeling God's presence all around, was a better time than most to share the vision of the South Side CDC project that Bree had discussed with her.

As she walked into the kitchen with Joel, he continued to voice some of his incomplete plans. Vera was there too, washing the serving dishes.

Vivian carefully brought up the idea of the mixed-income housing project; the vision of a diverse community that would offer inroads to home ownership for lower-income residents and space for seniors too; the possibility of acquiring tax incentives from the city. Vera was quick to register her excitement. And Joel was warming up to the idea too.

Craving an opportunity to think about creation rather than destruction, they discussed the ins and outs of building permits and Medicare, doing math on the back of a Lilith Magazine subscription insert that Vera pulled out of the recycling bin, too excited to even cross the room to retrieve a legal pad.

Scribbling and talking for hours until the sky changed colors, after all the other guests had returned home, Vivian thought that this might have been the most effective Beth Abraham committee meeting she had ever attended. They each left with their next steps. Vivian would call Bree the next day to start running the numbers. Joel would get some additional figures about the plot from Harry, and Vera would start drumming up support from others in the community.

"Now *this* project," Vera said. "*This* would contain the holy presence."

TWENTY-FIVE

"**M**MM," SHEILA SAID, breathing in the handful of rosemary she had just picked. "Smell this, baby." She reached over to Raymond.

As was the case on most Sunday afternoons in spring, the Weekses were in their backyard garden. Sheila harvested the early herbs while Raymond prepared the bed for their squash, turning the soil over and over. He leaned his shovel against the fence, twisted his torso in search of a comfortable position and inclined his head toward Sheila. "Yeah, honey, that smells good."

"Raymond Weeks." Sheila pursed her lips. "Will you please take a real sniff, maybe close your eyes or something?" She held the bunch close to his face without retreat. "I've worked damn hard on these herbs and you better appreciate them."

Raymond breathed in again, slowly. He smiled at her. "I can't wait to smother that on some chicken."

Sheila returned to her plot. Crouching down, she began pruning the bunches of lush mint, her face hidden below the wide brim of her hat.

"You thinking about the fire?" she asked.

Raymond remained still, gazing toward his vegetable beds, considering all the work yet to be done.

Sheila cut with more vigor at her plant. "Just talk to me about it."

Raymond turned toward her. "It's a sad thing, I get that. But when I was hanging around the synagogue on Friday, checking if people were okay, I kept hearing these whispers of antisemites and hate crimes and all that." Raymond shook his head, looking back at the neat row of basil. "I've been around these people for so long, and nothing bad ever seems to happen. What are they so afraid of?"

"Do you know for sure that it wasn't arson?" Sheila asked.

"No, but that seems unlikely, doesn't it? I mean, come on, honey." His words slowed. "*Who* would choose a synagogue on the East Side to set on fire, and not expect hell to pay?"

"Are you just mad that Joseph won't support Mac?" Sheila said.

"Yeah, I am."

"Well, that makes two of us, baby," Sheila said, "but that doesn't mean there was no wrongdoing here."

He picked some mint out of the basket where she had placed her yield and popped it into his mouth. "These people live in a bubble of protection. And we clearly don't have that luxury."

The sun above them was softening. Sheila adjusted her head to look at Raymond and avoid the glare. "But Ray, that doesn't mean bad things don't happen to White people. I've worked as a nurse long enough to know that."

"Whose side are you on anyway?" Raymond huffed. Sheila stared him down, and he knew not to extend that line of thinking.

"Fine, but do I have to care?" he said, a little louder this time. "Everyone's mourning and crying. But no one was hurt, and everyone gets to continue with their lives. And I'll bet the insurance they've got will mean they'll just build something better. That kind of thing would never happen here."

"So then stop complaining about *there* and do something *here*," Sheila said, turning toward their picnic table. It was strewn with Alex Santiago's campaign signs—vestiges of Mac's frequent door-knocking. After Freddie had introduced them at a community meeting, Mac had thrown himself into the mayoral election wholeheartedly. He was preaching the Alex Santiago gospel all over town.

In fact, a few days earlier, Mac had asked his parents if the campaign could use their house as a staging ground for weekend canvasses. Sheila was excited about the idea, pleased to think that Mac had actually gotten a taste for organizing from all those nurses' union meetings he sat through as a child. Raymond, on the other hand, was wary of inviting a bunch of strangers to hang around his house every weekend, no matter the cause. Even he had to admit, though, that the thought of

Mac following quite literally in his namesake's footsteps—door-to-door campaigning through his neighborhood—warmed his heart.

Raymond laughed. "Very slick." He walked toward the table and picked up a homemade lawn sign. "So, you're going to use my frustration to convince me to say yes to Mac, huh? Because Alex Santiago will solve all of our problems?"

"That's right, Ray. He's giving people hope," Sheila said, facing her herbs. "He's giving Mac hope."

Raymond sifted through more of the signs. Some were printed professionally. Many were just drawn by supporters with markers. It took him a minute to decipher that the messy O in Santiago on one of the posters was supposed to be a raised fist. "Fine, they can use our house," he said, "but they better clean all the dishes and not leave too much mess around."

Sheila sniffed her harvest and exhaled, absorbing her victory. Raymond let out a sound somewhere between a grunt and a laugh. He returned to the task at hand, retrieving his shovel and continuing to loosen the soil. Sheila always seemed to know best.

TWENTY-SIX

"**N**o need to mince words at a time like this," Harry began. "The damage to our synagogue is substantial. According to Chief Gonzalez, it's possible that some of the building will need to be demolished and rebuilt."

Harry had gathered the board for an emergency meeting at his home on the Tuesday following the fire. They sat in Harry's living room, which was more fragile than comfortable. All the furniture was black with sharp edges, and abstract glass sculptures were arranged like obstacles throughout the room.

"The fire department and police are going to stick around the building for the next week or two, continuing to put the pieces together," Harry continued. "In all likelihood, this was an accident of some kind, but it's possible that the fire was intentional. Now, I want to stress that it is very important for us to speak with a shared voice in this time of uncertainty. If we speculate, and spread speculated information, it could derail the investigation."

Shlomo Seidel, a board member who rarely attended meetings, spoke up. "Isn't it obvious? It was the antisemites. I mean, you see what's going on these days. The bomb threats, the shootings, the—"

"Shlomo, Shlomo," Harry interrupted, noticing that others around the room were nodding in support of Shlomo's claim. "Now look, the point of us being here is to ensure that we don't jump to conclusions, that we let the investigation play out and only speak when we know more about what happened on Friday night."

"But Harry, we don't have time," Shlomo said, his old, grey eyes bulging. His words lingered in the air. Harry often prepared containment plans for him at these meetings, planting others to respond quickly to Shlomo's conspiracy theories and unending monologues about the Jewish community's slow-moving demise. But Harry sensed that, this time, Shlomo was saying what others were thinking.

"Does anyone remember anything suspicious? Who else was in the building that night?" said another voice.

"There was nothing out of the ordinary," Harry said, trying to move the conversation forward. "The regulars, some younger folks."

"Ah yes!" Phil Katz said. "The young people. Who knows who they were? Maybe they did it!"

A few board members started to chuckle, then abruptly stopped. This was no time for jokes. A few looked to be considering the suggestion. Vivian grimaced in Harry's direction. As associate rabbi, she was not usually present at board meetings, but something he could not name had compelled Harry to invite her as he left Vera's a few nights earlier. Now he wished he hadn't.

"Again, it's not our job to solve this mystery," Harry said. "Let's leave the speculation to the professionals. They have been very helpful and are working to keep our community safe. We are here to develop a communication strategy and a plan for how we continue operating as a community."

"Hold on!" Phil Katz said, banging on the side table with enough force that the lampshade jumped. "I was at the scene a few days ago, when the police and fire department were investigating, and the custodian—I forget his name, it's, uh—"

"Raymond," Harry supplied.

"Right, Raymond," Phil continued. "He was there and was acting strange. It sounded like he was supposed to install a new oven or something and he didn't do it, without bothering to tell anyone. And then he left the room suddenly."

Chairs started to creak, giving voice to the discomfort in the room.

"Whoa, whoa, whoa, Phil. Stop right there," said Joseph, who did not often speak up at board meetings unless asked explicitly for his opinion. "We are not accusing anyone here. We are not going down rabbit holes of suspicion. You've all been watching too many crime shows. This ends now! We are here to get our message straight: The appropriate parties are looking into the fire. This process can take a while, and we will share what we learn with the community and the public when we know more."

While Joseph was speaking, Harry recalled Raymond's strange behavior in the kitchen earlier that week. It was true that Raymond had not mentioned that the new oven installation was delayed, and there was no way to prove he had actually written a note about it that got burned up. He had been quiet and left for no apparent reason in the middle of the fire chief's update. Maybe Joseph had shared their decision not to sign the letter about police funding and he was angry. Maybe Raymond....

"Harry, what's wrong?" another asked, as Harry's jaw clenched tightly. Despite his train of thought, Harry did not give more air to the group's suspicions. To his own suspicions. He would parse them later. "This is all just very stressful," he said.

"I fully agree with Rabbi Glass," Vivian started. "We have a big problem on our hands if the first people we suspect are within our own community. Like Raymond, who happens to be more entrenched in Beth Abraham than most of us, or like the new, younger guests visiting for the first time." She spread her arms out for emphasis, like wings. "How are we ever going to attract new people if we distrust those already here?"

Joseph's face was hardening as Vivian's speech progressed. "Viv—Rabbi Vivian, the point has been made. Let's move—"

"But are they?" Shlomo interrupted. "Part of our community, I mean."

"How can we trust them? We don't know them," Phil said, cultivating Shlomo's seed of mistrust.

"I can't believe—" Vivian started, then stopped, forcing the brakes on her rage.

"Can we please move on?" Vera stepped in.

Harry made an attempt to bring order back to the meeting. "Yes, let's. I want to reiterate that we will not be playing detective or prosecutor in this room, or in any other room for that matter. We are here to make a plan for our community. That is our only charge."

Harry moved on to the next agenda item though the weight of Shlomo's question, and the discussion preceding it, remained in the room like a ghost. "There are two practical matters to discuss. I have been in touch with many stakeholders in our community, many of whom have offered support through this difficult time. The building has suffered substantial damage. It is going to be a while before we pray in our synagogue again. The community center has given us a reduced rental rate so that we can host our services there for the time being. I propose that we accept their generous offer."

"Sure," someone said.

"That sounds fine," another board member added.

"But the community center is kind of far," Tamar Benayoun said.

"You drive on Shabbat, Tamar, don't you?" Shlomo sneered.

"I do," Tamar said, in a tone of defeat. "But I try to walk on most Shabbat evenings. And I know others who do the same. Beth Abraham is right in the center of our community; I think it would be difficult for people to get further downtown."

"Harry," Vivian said, clasping her hands together. "I'd like to propose that we do a bit more research on other possible spaces. The Unitarian congregation right down the block could be an option. I know one of the ministers there."

"We can't pray in a church," Shlomo said, looking toward Joseph. "Can we?"

"Actually, that's a bit more of a taboo than a decree, Shlomo," Joseph answered.

"I think it's worth looking into," Vera said. "The temporary space we choose should be holy. It should be conducive to prayer. And I would be happy to be on that subcommittee."

"Okay, Vera, but no Hindu temples with idols or anything," Harry said. Shlomo and Phil both snickered. "For now, we will meet at the community center, while a subcommittee researches other possible spaces more 'conducive to prayer.'" He mimed air quotes as he spoke the last phrase. "When they are ready with a proposal, we will call an executive board meeting so that we can make this decision efficiently." Everyone nodded their heads in agreement.

"All right, last order of business." Harry passed around a stack of papers containing graphs and numbers in small font. "Will Gould called me today. He let me know that his people are working on a new offer for the vacant plot. This new one would include his contractor doing all the repairs to *our* building, too, to fix the fire damage. Will said he'd even contact the insurance company and work with them to hammer out the numbers. But here are some preliminary figures."

The room was silent but for the sounds of papers shuffling.

"What a guy!" Phil Katz finally said.

"I'm a businessman," Harry continued, "and I'll tell you, coming back from the fire, dealing with the insurance, the

architects, the city and all the permits, the community members—on top of trying to make a deal for the land next door—
it's a lot of work. That's capacity, time and money we don't have.
Will is a member of this community. A leader! And he's also a
leader in this city, and he wants to do this right for us."

"Will's a businessman too," Vera said, her eyes fixed on the
proposal.

Harry ignored Vera's comment. "I move that, barring any
serious inconsistencies after seeing the full proposal, we award
Will and Riverside Developers the contracts for both projects."

"But, Harry," Joel said, shifting his focus between Vera and
Vivian, "we are getting closer to a proposal of our own. We are
working on it and plan to present it at the next regularly scheduled meeting in a few weeks. And it will have numbers and a
budget and everything."

"Joel, this is complicated stuff, at an even more complicated
time," Harry said, remembering their phone call that same
morning. Joel had peppered him with questions about the plot's
square footage and Beth Abraham's financials. He had fielded
them, certain that Joel and Vera's pet project would gain no
traction when compared to Will's offer. "Let's take the best deal
we can get here that requires the least amount of work. That's
a win in my book."

Joel whispered to Vera as others watched.

"There are obviously different emotions in the room,"
Joseph said, inserting himself. Everyone turned toward him.
"Why don't we all take some time to sleep on these conversations and think about what is best for Beth Abraham. We
have been through a lot and it's important that we conduct this

transition without too much more complication or *tsuris*. Let's revisit Will's proposal and the temporary space search at our next meeting, when we have more information and things have calmed down."

Harry thought of Will, anticipating another earful for not closing the deal. But he was too exhausted to push back. "Fine," Harry said, half relieved and half defeated.

Nods of agreement followed Joseph's suggestion, though not enough, technically, to constitute consensus. Amid the chaos and anxiety, Joseph's clarity seemed like enough.

"I just hope that the antisemites don't get us first," Shlomo said, barely audible. The others pretended they didn't hear.

"It's settled then," Harry said, slapping his hand on the table, adjourning the meeting.

TWENTY-SEVEN

V IVIAN WANTED TO put yesterday's board meeting behind
  her. She had been waiting to see Karla again ever since
leaving her apartment the morning after the fire. After strate-
gizing with Bree and Vera about the South Side CDC project
and then planning logistics for the upcoming Shabbat with the
ritual committee, it was finally time. She had even managed to
sneak a nap into her busy schedule. She and Karla were once
again meeting after nine, and Vivian wanted to be ready for
whatever the night might hold.

She longed to forget about the fire, about the toll it was
taking on her, on Joseph, on the community, for one night. She

had done some research and found good reviews for a live band that played soul music every Wednesday night at Club Savage downtown. She wanted to dance. Specifically, she wanted to dance with Karla, panel of judgmental rabbis be damned.

This time, Vivian was prepared. She wore a silk, button-down sleeveless top with skinny jeans, her sexy black boots, and dark red lipstick. As usual, she arrived a few minutes early and grabbed a seat at the bar. The music had started. Karla walked in, wearing ripped jeans and a tank top underneath a brown leather jacket. Vivian was struck by how gay she looked. Karla wore power suits well, but this outfit, this walk, this swagger, *this* was a different Karla.

Over the past few days, their exchanged texts had moved from consoling to flirtatious. In this moment, Vivian was feeling confident. She figured that the awkwardness of not knowing which type of greeting was appropriate was behind them, so as Karla approached, cutting through the crowd and the darkness, Vivian jumped up from her seat. Karla leaned in for a hug, her hand lingering on the small of Vivian's back.

"You clean up pretty well after a fire," Karla said.

"You look pretty hot yourself. I didn't know you owned jeans. If I hadn't unexpectedly spent the night at your house, I would have thought you slept in suits too."

"Unexpectedly?" Karla lifted an eyebrow. "Right, like you didn't just make the whole thing up to have an excuse to come over?" She covered her mouth with her hand. "Sorry, was that too soon? I mean, I know the fire was real and scary and—"

"For the sake of flirty banter," Vivian said, "you're doing just fine."

Karla laughed. "Let's get some drinks," she said, sitting down in an empty stool. "Do you want any food?"

"Not this time," Vivian said, remembering the delicious fried chicken she had eaten the previous week. "I've had dinner already." They ordered drinks and continued to talk, a bit louder than usual in order to compete with the music.

"So, how's the fallout from the fire been?" Karla said.

"We still don't know what happened," Vivian said, falling into a slouch. "It's possible that it was an accident. It's possible that it was antisemites. That's what everyone suspects anyway, even if they don't say it out loud. There's so much that points in that direction, except evidence."

Vivian rubbed her hands over her face, remembering her goals for the evening. "Actually, I'm not that interested in talking about work. Especially given how good you look. This is just not a scenario conducive to moping."

"I don't want to talk about work either," Karla said. "But one quick work update before we dive into date mode. Jeff is going to call you back in the next few days with possible dates for Mike to come visit. I just wanted you to be on the lookout, given everything else that's going on. All right, that's all I got. Let the date commence!"

"Okay!" Vivian said. "Let's see, let's see." She sipped her wine. "How about you tell me something I don't know about you? Something totally unrelated to work."

"Hmm." Karla took a swig of beer. "In high school, I won gold at the Rhode Island State Mathlete Championship."

"For real?" Vivian said loudly, both in surprise and to compete with the music's rising volume.

"That's right," Karla said. "But it's not actually something I bragged that much about. I was pretty quiet in high school and spent a lot of time alone. So, I figured I'd turn it into a competitive advantage."

Vivian swirled her glass around. "I wouldn't have expected you to be shy."

"When you start to realize you're queer and don't have anyone to talk to about it, solitude seems like a good option."

Vivian's knee touched Karla's, and she kept it there.

"What about you?" Karla asked.

Vivian stroked her chin theatrically. "I really love football."

Karla choked on her drink. "That's unexpected."

"My family was—is—obsessed with the Cincinnati Bengals," Vivian said. "We're religious about our religion and about our football team. But, unfortunately, all they've ever given us is disappointment and heartache."

"But isn't football, like, awful?" Karla asked. "The violence, the exploitation, the financial ties with the military?"

Vivian noticed that the rotating blue light had settled on Karla, adding emphasis to her disapproval. "I could give a whole sermon on the beauty of being connected to other people in Cincinnati, and how the players have been pushing the envelope and shining a light on institutional racism for an audience that wouldn't otherwise engage in that debate. But, honestly, given the amount of time and energy I've already invested, I just can't give it up. I love my team and I love football. We all have our vices, and now you know mine. Both of them."

Karla inched her whole body closer to Vivian's, and Vivian did the same. "Want to dance?" Karla asked.

Vivian was prepared for this, and yet self-consciousness around dancing with someone in public—dancing with a woman in public—pulsed through her tightening body. But she would not let on. This was going too well. She would just drink up the confidence oozing from Karla.

The dance floor was already packed. Vivian reminded herself that no one would stare, and that the rabbis were not real. She noticed other couples on the floor dancing close. Some looked sexy, some looked awkward. They all looked straight. But she was feeling the music, the lights were dim, and she was definitely tipsy. She wanted Karla.

They found a small opening on the dance floor. Each started dancing in her own space. Halfway through the first song, an Aretha Franklin classic, Vivian took the first step closer to Karla. Karla followed suit, putting her hands on Vivian's waist. They looked into each other's eyes. Their bodies glided together. It took a verse or two to find a shared rhythm, but they did, Karla with her shoulders moving sharply to the beat and Vivian letting her hands wander down Karla's arms. Vivian felt the music vibrate through her and rid her of whatever insecurities remained. They had chemistry and they both knew it.

They remained on the dance floor, entranced and tangled in each other. Every so often they would pull away, dance on their own. But their bodies kept calling the other back.

Vivian finally looked at her watch. It was almost midnight. She leaned over and said, "It's getting late. Thank you, this is exactly what I needed." She kissed Karla, almost without thinking. Karla gripped her wrist. They were still dancing. Karla broke the kiss and moved her mouth to Vivian's neck. Another charge ran through her body.

"Do you want any company tonight?" Karla asked. "You know, in case you still don't want to be alone."

Vivian did the calculus in her mind. She had banked some extra sleep and could make up more the next day. Her apartment was clean save a few books lying on the kitchen table that, if she were being honest, she had left out on purpose. And she was not actually in mourning, just shaken, just in need of comfort and distraction.

Vivian bit her lip. "Yes, I do think that would be the responsible choice."

TWENTY-EIGHT

B ETH ABRAHAM'S OFFICES were mostly untouched by the fire. Small amounts of smoke and water had reached them, but after an initial fumigation, the fire department had deemed the rooms safe. Joseph and Harry did not mind continuing their work surrounded by the rubble. That way, they were present and available for everyone coming through: city officials, the police and fire departments, the cleanup crew.

Vivian, however, could not bring herself to go back to the synagogue unless absolutely necessary. Instead, she accepted Lisa's invitation to work in an empty office at her church down the block.

The morning after her date with Karla, Vivian sauntered there, taking time to notice the hydrangeas blooming around her. She thought about Karla, about her body, their bodies first on the dance floor and then in her bed. She felt something close to calm.

First Parish of Providence was a multicolored stone building with just the right amount of ornament. Its handsome wooden doors, and the magnolia trees that framed them, glowed in the morning sun. It felt to Vivian like the right place to be that morning, in another holy space. Or maybe just with a friend to whom she could gush about Karla.

Vivian entered and made her way down the well-lit corridor of offices and Sunday school classrooms, a part of the church she had not seen before. She stopped to study the bulletin board. There was a poster recruiting congregants to tutor inmates in a nearby prison, another highlighting a speaker series on the spiritual implications of climate change, and a third publicizing something called "journey dance" that took place every Tuesday evening in the church's basement. She found Lisa's office and knocked on the open door.

"Good morning, Lisa."

Lisa looked up from her laptop in surprise and studied Vivian's face. "You look too happy to be leading a congregation through the aftermath of a traumatic fire," she said. "What's the deal?"

"Nothing. It's just a really nice day out," Vivian said, cupping her face in her hands. Lisa stared and crossed her arms. It did not take much for Vivian to start spilling. "Karla, this woman I'm seeing, who I met at the—"

"Viv, I know about Karla. Heather told me last week at the ecumenical breakfast," Lisa said.

"Ah. How topical," Vivian said, taking a seat opposite Lisa, right in the gleam of light entering through the side window. "We had our...third...date last night. We went dancing." Vivian's gaze drifted upward, trying to unsuccessfully repress her grin. "And then she stayed over."

Lisa shrieked with glee. "For some Bible study, I presume?"

"That's right. Bible study," Vivian said. "I know there's a lot to feel like crap about right now, but I just feel great."

"I'm so happy for you, Viv," Lisa said, closing the book she had been reading, an anthology of essays on liberation theology. She added it to the stack on the desk's corner. "Though you're going to have to get back to moping later today."

"I'll work on it."

"I'm glad to see you giddy like this," Lisa said.

"I'm not giddy," Vivian said, fidgeting with a rubber stress toy shaped like a chalice that she did not remember having picked up.

"Uh, you're giddy. Now tell me everything." Lisa closed her laptop and Vivian began recounting the details of the date.

Once caught up to the present, Vivian switched to a more serious tone. "There are still so many things to figure out. Today's task is searching for new venues for our services."

Vivian returned the stress toy to a small wicker basket overflowing with office paraphernalia. "I'm actually wondering if Beth Abraham could use your space for our Shabbat services. We could pay something, but obviously, the fire has left us in an uncertain financial situation. So, if you were able to give us the fellow-believers discount, that would be phenomenal."

Lisa leaned back in her chair. "You know my answer is yes, Viv, but it's not up to me. Whenever the board or Reverend Carrie has reached out to Joseph about collaboration, they've received a lukewarm response and no commitment. I'm sure they'll want to be charitable in the aftermath of the fire in some way, but there just isn't much of a relationship there."

"I know," Vivian said, thinking, again, that this chance to weave a wider web of community was why she was at Beth Abraham, why she was in Providence. "But perhaps that is one of the opportunities in this crisis. I'll talk to Joseph and the committee."

"All right," Lisa said. "But don't pick too many fights, Viv. Bree told me you're also doing some scheming with her about the vacant land on the synagogue's property. That's a lot of ground to cover at once."

"It might take a solid drive in the final two minutes of the game, but I think these are both achievable goals," Vivian said, swatting the air.

"Wow," Lisa said. "I have no idea what you just said, but your optimism, it's, uh, refreshing. You should hold late-night Bible study more often."

TWENTY-NINE

SANDWICHED BETWEEN A stack of papers and a family of noisy air filters, Harry sat in the main office, at the executive director's desk, keeping tabs on the ongoing investigation. Members of the fire department remained at the synagogue around the clock and often had questions. Harry decided he would be the one present to answer them. He had the time and he reckoned that he would do the best job.

He pored over the full proposal Will had sent him. Will would negotiate with the insurance company, secure city and state tax breaks and loans, and contract out the renovations to a company with low labor costs, thus ensuring that the dual project—building the condos from scratch *and* rebuilding half of the existing structure—would, even with the latter addition, still produce a significant surplus for Beth Abraham within four years. Harry already thought the world of Will, but for him, this sealed it: Will Gould was a master at cutting deals.

After examining the proposal and taking notes for his presentation at the next board meeting, Harry hunted the internet for relevant press coverage. He had been collecting all local news stories that mentioned the fire. The first article had come out the day after it happened, in the *Providence Chronicle*. It explained that the synagogue, built in the late 1800s by some of the first Jewish immigrants to the city, was one of Providence's oldest and most esteemed Jewish institutions. The write-up surveyed the damage and mentioned that the congregation's leadership was cooperating with police to investigate the possible cause, with no clear leads yet. Harry was pleased with the article. Those that followed in other local news outlets echoed the first.

Harry navigated to the website of the *Herald*, the town's more conservative newspaper, and read its follow-up article on the fire. Then he scrolled absentmindedly through the anonymous comments section. Someone called *GarryIllinois* had written, "That's what they get for killing Jesus."

As he kept scrolling he noticed more comments, posted by disembodied online personalities, that ranged from offensive to dangerous. Toward the bottom, he saw one from *Gr8American*. "It's a shame the whole Temple didn't burn down with all of you Jews in it." And then one from *JoJoRed*. "@Gr8American, that was the plan but guess I failed." And a smiley face.

Harry froze. Was this a confession?

He dashed over to Joseph's office a few doors down, bursting in without even a knock.

"Rabbi, there's something you need to see," Harry said to a startled Joseph. Planting himself behind the desk, Harry reached over him and took control of his computer.

He opened a blank tab in Internet Explorer and typed in the *Herald*'s homepage. Spotting the article link, he clicked on it and slowly scrolled down to the comments. He highlighted *JoJoRed*'s with the mouse.

Joseph adjusted his reading glasses as he studied the comments. His eyes grew bigger and bigger.

"We need to get the police back over here," Harry said.

"Okay, Harry," Joseph responded, remaining glued to the screen. "Make the call."

THIRTY

W HEN VIVIAN ARRIVED at the synagogue the next morning to retrieve a book before heading to First Parish, she
noticed activity near the back door. As she got closer, she spotted a huddle of people she did not recognize and large TV cameras on tripods. She could make out the figures of Joseph, Harry
Mermelstein and Will Gould. Walking through the parking lot,
she also noticed Mike McCann, in a tweed suit and burgundy
tie, with his blond hair unmoving in the wind. Standing next to
McCann was Police Chief Cal Thicke.

"One minute until showtime," shouted a woman in a blue
jacket adorned with a large, bright Channel Seven logo. Vivian was suspicious, of the cameras in particular. She stood at a

distance from the tangle of people, not knowing if she belonged closer. Then she saw that Karla was there too, whispering something in McCann's ear.

Bridget Black, the well-known face of Channel Seven news, opened her report. "Just days ago, while many in our local Jewish community were ushering in the holy Sabbath, a fire broke out at Congregation Beth Abraham. As violence against Jews has been on the rise around the country, there is reason to fear that this fire resulted from an act of hate, of antisemitism." She turned toward Joseph. "We are standing here with the rabbi of the community, Joseph Glass. Rabbi Glass, what is your community feeling right now?"

"We are scared, Bridget. It's the 21st century in America, and yet, there are still people who hate Jews and want to destroy us. We know that antisemitic individuals and groups have been emboldened both before and after this fire. We can't help but hear echoes of last year's brutal murder of our brothers and sisters a few hundred miles from here in their own synagogue."

Joseph's voice cracked. "I want to reiterate how much we appreciate the support of our local officials: the police, the fire department, the city council. They have all worked tirelessly with us over the past several days to clean up this mess and get to the bottom of it."

Bridget picked back up. "I'm also standing here with city councilor and mayoral candidate Mike McCann and with our chief of police, Cal Thicke. Councilor McCann, Chief Thicke, what is the City of Providence doing to respond?"

"Well, Bridget," McCann started, "we want to make it very clear: there is no place for hate in our city. Our Jewish brothers and sisters are valuable members of our community. We all know the fraught history, and we will not let it happen again. We will not tolerate any antisemitism."

"We will get to the bottom of this and heighten our vigilance in order to ensure that our Jewish neighbors feel safe here," added Chief Thicke, who was decked out in full uniform.

Bridget turned to Joseph. "How does it make you feel to hear that, Rabbi Glass?"

"Safe, and proud to live in Providence. Thank you, Chief Thicke and Councilor McCann." Joseph shook hands with the other two men.

Vivian stood still at the edge of the crowd, taking it all in, feeling weighted down by an influx of emotions: fear, anger, sadness. About what, toward whom, she could not yet say. She glanced at Karla, who looked like she had not moved a muscle since the broadcast began. She knew that Karla could see her too. Vivian felt something inserting itself between the two of them but could not name it. She fought back against the heaviness in her body, looked away from Karla, and walked off the synagogue grounds without her book.

THIRTY-ONE

Vivian arrived at Heather's just in time to watch the five o'clock newscast. Local TV news was not her usual cup of tea; nor, in fact, did she own a TV. But she had to see how Bridget Black's coverage looked to the rest of Providence (at least to all those over sixty).

"This is certainly a weird movie night, Viv," Heather said. "Want any popcorn?"

As she shifted her weight, dissatisfied with every position the normally cozy couch offered, Vivian looked at her phone. Again. Hours ago, Karla had texted her. *Hey. How was that for you?* She still could not bring herself to answer. She returned the phone to her pocket and waited for the report to begin.

They sat through a story about corruption at the State House and one about a slew of thefts on the South Side. Then the Beth Abraham segment played, just as Vivian had seen it in person.

"Heather, that wasn't great, right?" Vivian said, muting the television. "I'm not crazy? There's not even clear proof, just a vague wannabe confession from an anonymous troll on the internet."

"Viv, what happened to your community...." Heather spoke slowly, looking for the right words. "It's terrifying. Don't you realize that? And given that antisemitism is, um, trending—"

"Trending?"

"You know what I mean," Heather said. "I can understand why all those men would want to make a public declaration and seek out support. Though it's pretty messed up no one invited you to *that* meeting."

Vivian arose from the couch. "We get into this posture of victimhood, even when it might not be real," she said, pacing around Heather's living room. "But the outside world doesn't—"

"Stop trying to manage the outside world's reaction," Heather interrupted. "It's a scary and confusing time and there's a lot of work to do. But your responsibility is to your congregation."

"But when the people orchestrating the congregation's public image are Joseph and Harry, and probably Will Gould, too—"

"You have to climb out of this rabbit hole," Heather commanded. "Sit down and breathe."

Vivian sank into the couch and closed her eyes.

"But speaking of Will," Heather said, unable to take her own advice, "what was with his smirk in the background?"

"He loves flexing his muscles of power and connection," Vivian said. "I bet he made the press conference happen. In the meantime, he's trying to cut a deal for a piece of vacant land that the synagogue has owned for decades, so maybe he wanted to do a favor for—"

Vivian stopped mid-sentence as something on the muted screen caught her eye. "Hey, I think that's Mac, our custodian's son. What's he doing on the news?"

Heather retrieved the remote from Vivian's end of the couch and turned up the volume. Mac was standing in the center of a sizeable crowd next to Alex Santiago. "Tonight there has been another protest at this South Side police station," an anchor said.

The camera cut to Alex Santiago. "Enough is enough. Too many Black bodies have been harassed by the police in this city. We won't stand for it anymore."

The next frame focused on Mac, his face still discolored and bruised. "A few weeks ago, I rode my bike through a stop sign at this intersection. A cop stopped me, and without any warning, he threw me against his police car and beat me up."

Back to Alex Santiago. "Every Black resident has a story of police mistreatment like Mac's. And yet, as the city cuts funding for public education and affordable housing, the police budget goes up and they continue to wreak havoc on our community. But we, the taxpayers of Providence, pay their salaries, and it's time to reallocate our money—to take it out of policing and put it into services that actually benefit Black residents of Providence."

In the last shot of the segment, a reporter tried to get a comment from Cal Thicke as he left the station. "Chief Thicke, what do you make of this protest, of these demands?" the reporter asked, holding out his microphone and jogging to keep up as Thicke moved quickly through the crowd.

Cal Thicke speedily shimmied into his car, without saying a word.

When the piece ended, Heather turned off the TV. Vivian sat still.

"Yikes, Viv," Heather said, the remote frozen in her hand. "Now *that* was bad."

"So, when things get dicey, White Jews fawn over the police," Vivian said with her hands covering her face, "while young Black people are harassed by them?"

THIRTY-TWO

VIVIAN KNEW JOSEPH would be in his office. He had barely left all week. While she drove the ten minutes from Heather's, she thought about what she would say, what words she could string together that would adequately convey her anger, her confusion, her....

She had learned to translate her critiques into opportunities, rather than threats, when negotiating with Joseph. But this was different. This moment was about everything. And everything was hard to untangle.

Vivian thought back to their last encounter. For days now, Joseph had been collecting the burnt books and loose pages—from Hebrew school classrooms, the sanctuary, the lawn where they had blown and scattered. She had watched him from a distance, several times, as he gently kissed each and placed it atop one of the countless piles that swelled in the hallway. Pages of old siddurim no longer in use, books of midrash, of philosophy, biographies of famous Jewish athletes, teachings for children about Shabbat. All still damp and fragile from the firehoses. Vivian thought of them as Beth Abraham's very own *geniza* of salvaged sacred texts, distinct layers that together told the story of the congregation.

On that afternoon a few days earlier, she had found him hunched over one of the piles, trying to blow the pages dry with his breath. He told her that the cleanup company had mistakenly disposed of the mountain he had already collected, and he bemoaned their profane resting place.

Vivian had not remembered seeing Joseph like this, without a plan and so small. She grabbed a shovel from the maintenance closet and a short stack from the paper remnants. She told Joseph to follow her and walked out of the building.

Somewhere between the blackened classrooms and the unused plot, with their one tool and four hands, they dug a hole in the soft earth and buried their small bundle. High Holiday prayer books, collections of commentary and instruction, loose pages of an apple-cake recipe.

Tonight, though, Vivian found Joseph surrounded by quite intact books. He was at his desk, writing notes with purpose. She walked into his office without a greeting.

"Joseph, why did we have to go and alert the presses this morning?"

He looked up, startled and exhausted.

"Half our building has been destroyed, Vivian," he said, massaging his forehead. "Congregants were traumatized. We could have all been killed. We have to make it clear that no antisemitism will be tolerated. And we need local officials on our side here."

"But we aren't even sure what happened."

Joseph recounted the latest theory. Revisiting the scene after the discovery of *JoJoRed*'s confession, Fire Chief Gonzalez had hypothesized that the kitchen windows could have shattered when someone outside the building threw in a small explosive device, rather than having broken from the pressure of an internal fire.

"We are close to sure," Joseph said. "We practically have a confession. And, regardless, we can't stand by. These kinds of threats are being made all over the country. I don't have to remind you about the shooting last year, about the stories we hear weekly of desecrated shuls and cemeteries. We are lucky to have the right connections so we can act fast and prevent more damage."

"But that's the problem. We are moving *too* fast, we need to slow down," Vivian said, approaching his desk and slapping her hand down onto it. "We need to take stock of the situation, not just respond out of fear."

"That's how we survive, Vivian. That's how we have always survived. By acting with clarity. When we haven't in the past, it hasn't worked out so well for us."

Vivian had learned not to engage Joseph's oblique references to the Holocaust.

"But that doesn't have to mean overnight. We can breathe

and take our time and weigh out all the options. Let's let this investigation play out so we can be sure what happened."

"Vivian, I appreciate the vitality you bring to this community," Joseph said, standing up from his desk. "We need new energy, new perspectives, new tunes. But you grew up in a different time. You don't get it. You don't get what it was like to have experienced such unfathomable cruelty or to have heard firsthand accounts throughout your whole childhood. These threats have dire consequences. This is a moment to yield to your elders."

Vivian turned away, facing Joseph's bookshelf. Her eyes fell on what Joseph called "the Holocaust shelf." Victor Frankl, Elie Wiesel, Anne Frank. Their spines were worn. Somehow, we have developed warring instincts, she thought.

"I try to get it, Joseph. I know the threats are serious. I know this is how it starts. That it's already started." Vivian paused wondering what she meant by *it*. "But if you really want this community to stay alive," she continued, "the Jewish people to adjust accordingly to the times, we can't just revert back to our old instincts when it really matters. We'll never grow that way."

Joseph looked down toward his book, and Vivian kept going.

"Joseph, there are a lot of people who mistrust our police force. If we continue to raise them up as our protectors without any critique, we are showing that we don't care about them—about Mac, about Raymond." She thought of Flora, the young woman who had been there the night of the fire. "About Jews of Color who might find their way here," she added.

"Vivian, of course we care about Raymond. Of course we want our community to be welcoming." Joseph stroked his beard, searching for his next words. "It's just that, sometimes, we have to make choices."

Vivian could not summon a response. She turned toward the office door.

"Vivian, hold on," Joseph spoke up, catching her before she left the room. "There's uh, there's one other thing we need to talk about. I know the timing isn't great, but...." He sighed. "We have to bury this other housing proposal and give Will both contracts. We're in bad financial shape, you know, along with everything else. And we just need to resolve this piece and move forward with some, um, security."

Vivian looked back at Joseph, whose face was turned away from her, toward the window. She thought of Will, standing in the background on the TV screen. So that's why he was grinning. He could already taste victory.

Security. Vivian rolled the word around in her mind as she left the building, not looking back. Stepping out onto Banks Street, she noticed the two police cars that now seemed permanently parked out front. *Security.* Why were people acting like there was only so much of it to go around?

THIRTY-THREE

VIVIAN HAD REPLAYED the last time she intentionally saw Karla over and over in her memory. Dancing, kissing, waking up together. But now, walking toward Karla's apartment, Vivian had no idea what she wanted—from their date, from Karla.

The front door was unlocked. Vivian could hear a sizzle coming from the kitchen. She followed the sound and found Karla there.

"I hope you like spicy food," Karla said. "I'm cooking us some enchiladas." Vivian could hear uncertainty in her voice.

"That sounds fine," Vivian said.

"You okay?" Karla asked.

"Fine," she replied in the same tone.

"I don't think I've ever heard you use the word *fine*," Karla said, putting down her spatula and looking at Vivian. "Let's talk. Why haven't you responded to my texts?"

Vivian folded her arms and leaned against the island, on the threshold between the living room and the kitchen. "What was Mike trying to pull yesterday?"

"Mike's trying to do the right thing here," Karla said, unconsciously mirroring Vivian's pose. "It wasn't even his idea, it was Will's."

"Mike is using us for his political gain," Vivian said. "And you're helping him. There is no proof yet, and his politicking is fueling my community's fears."

"He's still making a strong point to the Jewish community that he'll protect you, us," Karla said, twisting away from Vivian to rummage through her spice cabinet. "That's progress, right?"

"We don't only need protection." Vivian's voice was rising. "We have all kinds of protections and privileges today, Karla. And it's so hard for us to realize it because we are always stuck thinking that we are victims. And Mike is making that worse right now. Come on, you're Jewish. Have you ever felt unsafe as a Jew?"

Vivian repeated the question to herself. Recently, she had started to feel unsafe in her Jewish skin, for the first time. She felt it walking into services at Beth Abraham the Shabbat after the shooting the previous year, and the Shabbat that followed, and the one after that. Over time, the tightness in her body softened. She barely thought about it anymore. Until the fire.

Locating the black pepper, Karla slammed the cabinet door. "No, but I'm not really Jewish, I just, you know, blend in."

Suddenly there was a loud beeping noise. Steam from the sautéing vegetables had set off the smoke alarm. "Shit," Karla said. She turned off the stove and pushed a stool over to the smoke detector in the corner of the room.

"Need any help?" Vivian said, jolted out of her train of thought. Karla ignored her and kept fidgeting with the alarm.

The beeping stopped, and Karla kept on moving, transferring the vegetables into a ceramic bowl on the counter.

"Can you start folding the tortillas?" she asked Vivian, not looking directly at her. She returned to her second pan. Spiced black beans.

Vivian placed the veggies next to a plate of grated cheese, and she started to lay out the tortillas. For a moment, they were simply cooking together on a normal date.

"You know, Karla, most of us White Jews blend in," Vivian said, choosing confrontation over the silence. "You and I have benefitted from the same process of assimilation. That's why we feel secure." She stopped folding. "*Mostly* secure," she edited. "Until we get used as a political bargaining chip and then pitted against other groups."

"The calculus here makes sense, okay?" Karla said. "For the sake of all these relationships, standing with your community against antisemitism and seeing this investigation through just makes sense."

"Is that all this is about for you?" Vivian asked. "Making sure you still get Will Gould's money?"

Karla transferred the beans into a bowl and set it down in

Vivian's assembly line. "Like it or not, to get into office and have an impact, we need him on our side."

Vivian stopped filling tortillas and looked straight at Karla. "That's not centrism, or whatever you call it. That's just selling out."

"This is what we have to do to get into a position to do more good," Karla said, looking away from Vivian. "This is what *I* have to do to get into a position to do more good."

"But at what cost?" Vivian shouted, slapping the counter and barely avoiding upsetting the bowl of beans. "And if you make these concessions now, what will you give up down the line?"

"We can't all be ideological purists. Especially when the stakes are so high. I mean, this isn't a congregation, Vivian, this is the future of our city we are talking about."

Vivian stared back at Karla. "This is not about stakes. This is about your own priorities and choices. You know Margaret Heath isn't going to run the city into the ground. It's just that if she wins, you've got a higher mountain to climb."

"I'm sorry," Karla said. "Mike has made up his mind." She looked toward the counter at the unfinished enchiladas.

"If that's the only possibility you see, I don't know what else to say." Tears welled up in Vivian's eyes. "It seems like we're not on the same team here."

"What are you trying to say?"

"That I don't know if I can stick around and see where this goes while you and your boss fan the flames of fear and division in my community," Vivian replied.

"So, we're done?" Karla's voice cracked.

Vivian rubbed her temples. "Maybe. I don't know. Everything is so confusing right now."

"Just let things be a little messy."

"There's enough mess to deal with."

Karla looked around at all the artifacts of the unfinished dinner project. She reached for Vivian's hand. "Come on, don't—"

Vivian pulled back her hand and, for what seemed like the hundredth time in the past few days, walked away unsure if she wanted to cry or scream.

THIRTY-FOUR

CHIEF THICKE AND members of the Rhode Island State Police's cybersecurity department found themselves in front of a shabby split level on a sparsely populated street. The team had sifted through *JoJoRed*'s online activity and conducted an extensive search for his IP address. The devices he used had led them to this spot, one hour south of the city.

A middle-aged White woman with wavy blonde hair and tired eyes opened the door. She jumped at the sight of the police. "We're here to ask your son some questions about an incident that he may have been involved in," Chief Thicke said, holding up a search warrant. She stared at the document and seemed to hesitate about what to do.

"Ma'am?" Thicke prompted her. She howled down the hall-way, and a diminutive teenager stepped into view.

Joey Forsyth's computer was filled, they found, with par-aphernalia from a hate group called the Guardians of Amer-ica. The cybersecurity team recognized the name immediately from research the FBI shared with local law enforcement. Apparently, chatroom activity associated with the Guardians of America had spiked in recent months. Calling Jews "Amer-ica's disease," "a disease that needs curing," was a recurring preoccupation.

The police spent several hours trying to determine Joey's relationship to the fire at Beth Abraham. That Friday evening, he had been with his mom and sister, watching two of the Ter-minator movies back to back. Joey's stunned mother confirmed it, sharing selfies they'd taken during the movie marathon.

Chief Thicke found Joey's motivations unclear. What he and his team could gather was that Joey was trying to impress the other Guardians, as he called them, with his online con-fession. And since then, his engagement, the caliber of chats he was welcomed into, had risen. The officers questioned him about his ideology, his actions, trying to ascertain what kind of threat he posed, but Joey never articulated anything coherent.

"I got bored of Minecraft, and I moved onto Guardians," he said, shrugging.

The cops seized Joey's computer. One notified Joey's prin-cipal, asking her to keep tabs on him. They still had a few more calls to make to confirm Joey's alibi, but it was quite clear that, while Joey's online confession was deeply troubling, he had not, in fact, set Beth Abraham on fire.

Chief Thicke stepped outside and called Harry to share the news.

"But Cal," Harry said, "this was a real, live threat. And there are more out there. Doesn't that prove this was a hate crime?"

"It's still a possibility," the chief said. "But there isn't any actual evidence."

"Of course there is," Harry said. "There's a clear pattern of attacks on Jewish institutions. *That's* evidence."

"That's not enough to build a charge on, Harry." Thicke hung up and returned to the living room, where his team was wrapping up. He noticed that Joey's pajama bottoms were patterned with SpongeBob SquarePants. It made him think of his own kids. They loved YouTube clips of that show.

"All right, boys, let's head on home," he said in a low voice.

The search for answers was back on.

THIRTY-FIVE

T HE WALLS OF the synagogue's kitchen had dried, the ash had settled, the debris had been swept up. Members of the Providence Fire Department had a fresh look at ground zero. A few of them hovered over the oven. The wires were a mess, some disconnected, some fused together. Crouching down to get a closer look, they discussed the possibilities. Tampering. Damage from the fire.

Fire Chief Marco Gonzalez stood behind the cluster of firefighters, staring a few feet above the focal point of the others. He called over the rest of the cleanup crew. "You see this pattern, fellas?" Rising vertically over the oven's carcass, a V-shaped pattern of soot crawled up the wall. Gonzalez drew closer and lightly traced the smear with his fingers, not quite touching it. It was slender and the darkest shade of black.

"That's it," he continued. "That's where the fire started. You can tell because of how narrow it is, and because the pattern has stuck while a lot of the other filth and ash splattered from the water pressure."

"What about the smashed windows, Chief?" one of the firefighters said. "Couldn't it still be the case that someone threw a device in from the outside?"

"It doesn't add up, Manny," Gonzalez answered. "The impact wasn't intense enough. We'd see dents, we'd see more dismembered appliances, more shrapnel, whereas the windows could have easily cracked from the fire's pressure."

"That does fit better with how the broken glass was distributed, mostly outside and not in here," another firefighter said. "And there's still the issue of the smoke alarms."

The fire chief paced around the kitchen. "But we've got a gift here, boys." He traced the V above the oven one more time. He stepped back and stared at the meeting point between the wall and ceiling. "I think this was an inside job. Someone disconnected the alarms in the kitchen and the hallway and tampered with the oven to make it look like an accident."

"So it had to be someone in the building?" Manny asked.

"I think so."

Gonzalez walked with purpose toward Harry's office. He had been frustrated by the Channel Seven news spectacle, which had occurred despite his protest that their investigation of the building was still incomplete. He entered without knocking.

"Harry, we think someone who was inside the building that

night started this fire. You should gather a list of all the people who were here for the police."

Harry stared blankly at the fire chief. Gonzalez repeated himself.

"You mean to tell me someone in our own congregation did this?" Harry finally said. Gonzalez nodded.

"No, no, no." Harry waved his hands. "That can't be. How could...? I mean, we're all...."

"Harry, no one ever wants to believe that it's one of theirs who did it. But after three decades of this work, I'm never surprised anymore. All people—bad people, good people, mediocre people—are capable of causing a whole lot of damage."

After sharing some more details about their findings, Chief Gonzalez left Harry's office, returning to the kitchen. Harry sat in his chair, stunned, listening to the ticking of the clock. When the chief had come to find him, he had been digging through the Guardians of America chatrooms, still trying to make sense of the news that *JoJoRed* was not to blame. The hate he found there, the lethal antisemitism, made it clear that Joey Forsyth was the tip of a deep disgusting iceberg.

A loud thud from the direction of the kitchen jolted him out of his trance. He started composing the list of everyone he remembered seeing in the building that night. Since the fire, the light security detail they had hired had not reported anything or anyone strange. He would check with Joseph and the others.

Harry rose from his desk and marched through the building in search of clues, matching his steps to the pace of his racing mind. *So many people hate us. And yet it was someone who walked through these halls, maybe even prayed with us, who decided to set the whole place on fire?*

On his second lap through the synagogue, he noticed Raymond sweeping one of the classrooms. Harry stopped in the doorway. He thought back to the accusations that Shlomo had started to make against Raymond at the board meeting, which Harry himself had quickly shut down. Raymond, who had been a well-performing employee for several decades. Raymond, who seemed distracted when the police and fire departments began the investigation. Raymond, who never saw to it that the new oven was installed. Raymond, who was probably angry at Joseph, at him—maybe even at everyone—for refusing to sign that stupid letter picking a fight with the police.

Harry approached and patted Raymond on the back, startling him.

"Didn't mean to scare you," Harry said. Raymond turned and faced him.

"We learned more about the fire today. The fire chief says he's sure it must have been started by someone who had access to the kitchen. Do you have any idea how that could have happened?"

"No, sir." Raymond gripped his broom tightly.

"It's just—there aren't many people on that list, and I want to make sure that...."

Harry was not sure how to finish his sentence. His eyes fell on a smoke-damaged poster behind Raymond that was barely legible. *How do you tikkun olam?* The O in *olam* was an image of Earth, with smiling stick-figure children holding hands in a circle around it. Harry noticed Raymond studying his face, and his cheeks flushed. He still could not locate the right words, so it was Raymond who broke the silence.

"Are you saying you think I did this?" he stated, seeming to grow more distant with each word.

"No. Not exactly." Harry cleared his throat. "I'm just exploring the different possibilities."

Raymond breathed heavily, leaving space for Harry to catch himself. But Harry said nothing.

"I should have done this a long time ago," Raymond said, handing his broom to Harry. Harry did not reach out for it, and it dropped on the ground, right at his feet. Raymond removed the keys that hung from his belt and dropped them, too. Their jangling echoed through the room.

"I quit." Without hesitation, Raymond left the classroom. He strode down the charred hallway and out of Harry's sight.

THIRTY-SIX

"**U**NLIMITED MIMOSAS ON me, Viv. Looks like this fire has taken a toll on you," Lisa said, rubbing Vivian's back as she slid into their usual booth at the Hideaway.

"I don't even know where to start," Vivian said. "It's not just that. I mean, don't get me wrong, shepherding a community in the aftermath of a fire is exhausting, but the past few weeks have unearthed so many other questions about who we are." She paused. "And then I might have ended things with Karla because of Mike's publicity stunt."

"What?" Heather choked on her water. "Sorry. I know you just said something pretty deep about your community or whatever, but let's start there. You and the campaign manager are done? Just like that?"

"I don't know," Vivian said, running her hands through her hair. "But that's not a very helpful response, Heather."

"Sorry," Heather said. "I'm just very invested in your love life."

"Well, Viv, where do you want to start?" Lisa said. "What do you need from us?"

"I just need you to tell me that while I feel like shit now, things will get better, maybe not right away but down the road. The synagogue will get rebuilt, I'll find lasting and loving partnership, and the soul of the Jewish people isn't totally lost in a dark forest of self-obsession."

The waiter hesitantly approached the group to take their orders.

Before he could speak, Heather did. "Two mimosas, and blueberry pancakes all around," she said, shooing him away and getting back to the business at hand.

"Wow, that's...a lot." Heather struggled to find the right words and then gave up. "Lisa, you got anything?"

"We are here for you," Lisa said. "Your community just had a traumatic experience. *You* just had a traumatic experience. That takes time to heal."

Heather nodded in approval. "Exactly what I meant to say."

"I know the threats of antisemitism are real," Vivian continued. "I'm trying to get how that deeply impacts my congregants, and Joseph. But they've got to loosen their grip on the idea that it's the only enemy that we are up against. It's entrenched in their—in our—bones. It's visceral. And it renders us incapable of seeing what others are up against and need."

Vivian paused. "Raymond, our custodian, just quit, because

when it turned out that maybe the fire was started by someone inside the building and not by anonymous antisemites, Harry immediately accused him. Our one employee who's not Jewish, who's Black, and who's worked there for I don't know how long." She started to cry. "I don't know who we are right now. When we most need to open ourselves up, we close ourselves off."

"If it helps to know, your community does not have a monopoly on missing the mark, Viv," Lisa said, leaning in closer. "My predominantly White congregation seems to have no problem singing traditional Black spirituals without acknowledging that our own original church building was funded by a family who made their fortune by enslaving people. I tried facilitating a workshop about this last week, and let's just say it did not go over well. And it's not completely their—I mean *our* fault, Viv. There are other forces here. More sinister forces in the background setting the stage, like White supremacy and—"

Vivian's eyes widened. "What did you say?"

"Sorry," Lisa said, confused. "I know that term can be a trigger for—"

"No, before that."

"That there are always forces hovering over us that we don't see that shape our reality," Lisa repeated. "And yet we get distracted and blame each other, or whoever is easy to point fingers at."

The waiter returned with their pancakes, set them down and quickly disappeared.

"Oh my god," Vivian said, wiping her eyes and sitting up straight. "I think I know who started the fire." She poured syrup over her breakfast. "It's the force hovering over us that shapes our reality."

"Hold on, Viv. I'm confused." Heather said. "Are we trying to assure you that this will pass and everything will be okay? Or do you actually need to spiral right now? Spiraling can be healthy under the right circumstances."

"No, no," Vivian said, straightening out the wrinkles in her plaid shirt. "Thank you for your love and reassurance, but I'm okay now. Think about it! Who is the force in the background shaping reality?"

"God?" Lisa said.

"Well, yeah, but I mean a wicked force."

"Not to go off on a tangent," Lisa said, "but my theology doesn't preclude the divine force from being cruel at times."

Heather elbowed her. "And we will get right back to that important topic at our next brunch, won't we, Lisa? Viv, you were saying?"

"I have a thought," Vivian said, pulling a pen and crumpled receipt out of her tote bag. "But I need to do some research, to be sure before I say anything," she continued as she scribbled some notes.

"You're not going to tell us?" Heather said.

"Not yet."

They pressed her for information, but she would not budge.

"Fine, then at least tell us about the breakup," Heather said. "What happened?"

"We didn't break up. We just left things, you know, messy." Vivian said, remembering how tight her body had been when she walked out on Karla. "She stood by and helped McCann use the synagogue to score points for the campaign."

"So, what now?" Lisa said.

"I don't know. I really liked her. I *do* really like her."

"Then don't end it. Just give things time to work themselves out," Heather said, chewing a big bite of pancake.

"But she used us. She used me!"

"Viv," Lisa said, "maybe Karla deserves some compassion. It sounds pretty complicated, even if you think it's all so clear."

Vivian laughed.

"What's so funny?" Lisa asked.

"Karla once said something similar to me. She was criticizing the ideological purity of the prophets."

"Wow, that's what you talk about on your dates?" Heather chuckled. "Are you freaking kidding me? She is a keeper!"

"Anyway, I told her that wasn't the tradition we carry on today. We struggle and weigh out different factors in order to arrive at hard decisions." Vivian groaned and then threw up her hands. "Oh no. Did I just take her side? But still, she had a big hand in a political stunt that—"

"Give it time," Lisa interrupted, putting her hand on Vivian's arm.

They lingered at the Hideaway, workshopping Lisa's next sermon and how she would approach Carrie to ask if First Parish could cheaply rent prayer space to Beth Abraham. Walking her friends out to their cars in the parking lot, Vivian hugged Lisa, then Heather. She let out a small laugh.

"Thanks for listening to me. Turns out one brunch with some wise women actually can address all of your major crises."

THIRTY-SEVEN

"HEY, KARLA. DO we still need to schedule a visit to that synagogue, or did the press coverage seal the deal?" shouted Jeff, McCann's scheduler, from across the crowded office. The campaign was headquartered in a sprawling strip mall on the outskirts of Providence. Everyone except Mike, who had his own cubicle in the corner, sat at folding tables piled high with pamphlets and buttons.

"I think we're set, Jeff," Karla said, in a monotone. "Let's work on the Catholics and the soccer moms this week." The question brought back all of the feelings she was trying to suppress.

The night Vivian left, Karla had slammed the door shut and shouted at the air. For the next few days, there was a scream at the back of her throat, threatening to come out. At first, she thought it was just a tangle of sadness and anger toward Vivian for overreacting. But as it settled into what felt like a peach pit, it also seemed like doubt about the strength of her own position.

Karla knew that working for Mike McCann was not her dream job, but it offered good experience and useful connections. And Mike really listened to her. He often spoke her words and ideas, messages of centrism sprinkled with sincere progressivism. But now she was beginning to feel her college-aged self judging her current self. While she could easily dismiss that younger voice—it positively dripped with self-righteousness—she nonetheless longed for its certainty. It probably hadn't helped that, on the night of the maybe-breakup, she had binge-watched the first season of *The West Wing*. She was jealous of the clarity and conviction that President Bartlett's staff carried with them into their work.

But she knew she had to pull it together, to focus. Alex Santiago and Margaret Heath were both gaining steam with their own constituencies. Santiago was awakening millennials and somewhat successfully convincing Providence's Black and Latinx communities that he could actually change big systems for the better. The protests in front of the police station had stayed in the news, on social media and on the minds of many residents. The *Chronicle* was running a series recounting stories of police misconduct against residents, including Mac Weeks, and Santiago was frequently quoted.

Heath's campaign, meanwhile, was publicizing the bold affordable-housing guidelines for all new development that she would fight for as mayor. Though a group of developers, behind the innocuous name "Coalition for a Better Providence," had invested in an assortment of negative ads accusing her of raising rents for everyone, Heath's numbers continued to rise as she made the rounds, meeting new community groups and saying yes to every interview.

Mike, meanwhile, was stagnating, relying on the same messages and banking on union support and mid- to large-level donations to maintain his shrinking lead. But Karla was committed to her work, to Mike, and she remained skeptical of either Santiago or Heath's ability to convince the electorate that their flashy plans could become policy.

As Karla was reviewing talking points for the events of the day, the campaign's finance director, Jamie, abruptly shouted her name from across the open office.

"Yeah?"

"You know Gould, that big developer who pledged $20,000?" Jamie asked.

"What about him?"

"His check just bounced," Jamie said. "What gives?"

"That's strange. I'll ask Mike when he gets in," Karla answered.

A few minutes later, McCann walked in. He often arrived about an hour after Karla and the others. Most mornings, she did not let it get to her, but she was already feeling irritable.

After giving Mike a minute to settle in, she went over to his cubicle for his daily briefing: the day's events (a coffee klatch with another seniors' group), press engagements (an interview on local public radio about the school district's budget), and policy updates (the latest on activists' efforts to demand increased property taxes on corporate development). She saved the news about Will Gould's check for the end.

"How is that possible?" he said, jumping up from his chair.

"I don't know, Mike."

He slammed his hands on his desk, which was bare in comparison to the others, then rubbed his face trying to calm his frustration. "I'll give his money guy a call."

Karla left him in his cube. She heard the dial tone for a few seconds, then aggressive dialing.

"Jay? Good morning. It's Mike McCann. My team just let me know that Will's check bounced. I'm guessing there is some kind of mistake. Could you look into that?"

Karla could not make out what Money Guy was saying on the other line, but in response Mike's voice rose in unmasked irritation.

"What do you mean?" he demanded. "But we need that money."

He lowered his voice, and Karla could barely make out him saying, "I thought we had a deal. He can't just—" Then he was audible again. "Okay, but it better be soon, Jay."

A few more seconds passed.

"Sorry, I didn't mean—fine, talk soon." He slammed the phone down.

Karla could hear Mike pacing and breathing heavily in the small space of his cube.

"It's time for the coffee klatch, Mike. We got to go," she shouted.

"Give me a minute," Mike snapped.

Through the makeshift wall, Karla could hear Mike tearing

up a piece of paper and then jamming something into his trash can, which rattled from the impact. He emerged from the cubicle.

"I got to take a leak. Then we'll go mingle with the old fogies," Mike said, dashing toward the bathroom.

Curiosity overtook Karla. She walked over to his cube, scanned to make sure no one was watching, then ducked in and pulled the torn pieces of paper from Mike's trash can. She laid them out on his bare desk and pieced them together like a puzzle. When she had finished, she found herself staring at a building permit from the City of Providence, signed by the Director of Inspectional Services, whose sloppy signature Karla couldn't make out. But the second signature was unmistakable. *Mayor Pro Tempore, Michael L. McCann.* The document concerned 24-28 Banks Street, the vacant property next to Beth Abraham. It was issued to Riverside Developers. In March. Two months ago.

Karla could hear the faint sound of the toilet flushing. She threw the pieces into the trash can, making it back to her desk just as the bathroom door swung open.

"All right, let's get this shit over with," Mike said with a scowl. He turned toward the door, expecting Karla to follow right behind him. And she did.

THIRTY-EIGHT

A FTER BRUNCH, VIVIAN detoured from her usual route and set out down less recognizable streets, trying to make sense of it all. Clouds had moved in, but the rain had not yet come. Her thoughts had turned to Raymond again. What's the etiquette for this moment—would the pharmacy carry a card that says "I'm sorry you lost your job?" or "I'm sorry you were pushed to quit after several decades by a racist Board president. Better luck next lifetime?"

Vivian's phone buzzed, interrupting her thoughts.

It was a text from Karla. Karla, whom she hadn't spoken to for a week; Karla, the thought of whom still made Vivian's whole body feel warm.

You should look into WG's business dealings, the message said. *Some things aren't adding up on your vacant property.*

Right, Will Gould. The other person she could not stop thinking about. Will, who always called the shots, even when he was not in the room; Will, who wore a smug grin in the background of the Channel Seven news coverage, as if he were untouchable even in the midst of destruction; Will, who had everyone in the city wrapped around his finger; Will, who was on vacation the night of the fire; Will, who, she was sure, still somehow started it.

And now, Vivian had Karla to think of. That she had become quite used to, wavering between wanting her and being enraged at her. Vivian stopped in the middle of the sidewalk, typing her response. *Thanks.* No. *Thank you*, she amended, wondering if that extra tinge of formality suited the situation better. She considered telling Karla how she was feeling, that she may have overreacted. But Karla had still not addressed what had happened, what she had done. There had been no apology, no nothing. And Karla *was* the one who needed to apologize. Vivian worried that Karla could sense her hesitation through the hovering response bubble in the conversation. *Thanks, Karla. I'll do that*, she finally wrote back.

She hurried back toward her apartment just as a steady drizzle began. She opened her laptop and did a Google search for news about Riverside Developers. There was not much recent coverage—a plot of land acquired here, a ribbon-cutting there. She kept scrolling. Finally, on the second page of search results, an article with the word "questionable" in its headline jumped out at her. Bingo!

The piece, published seven years earlier, described several building-trades unions' complaints against Riverside's compensation policies. She then spotted a second article, printed a few years later, that raised questions about how the company secured approval for a condo development right next to protected historical properties. But Vivian could not find any follow-up coverage on either story. The same reporter, Ty McReedy at the *Chronicle*, had written both.

Vivian's adrenaline overcame her fear. She found a number for the *Chronicle*'s news desk and immediately dialed it. A polite operator put her through to McReedy.

"Talk to me," he greeted her.

"Hi, I'm Rabbi Vivian Green from Congregation Beth Abraham."

"What can I do for you?" he asked. "Oh wait. Is that the church, I mean synagogue, the one the antisemites set on fire?"

"Yes, I mean, there was a fire, but we don't—" Vivian stopped herself, realizing this was not the moment to unpack all the complexities of intergenerational trauma and the array of potential causes of fires unrelated to arson. "You can imagine that our community is dealing with a lot. But I'm actually calling about some articles you wrote years back, about potential foul play by Riverside Developers."

"Uh, yeah?"

"Was there any follow-up? Are there still live concerns about their business practices? My congregation is likely contracting with them, and I wanted to—"

"Listen, I can't really talk about this. You should take it up with my editor, Ernest Calhoun." Without offering to connect her, Ty hung up.

Vivian redialed her friend the operator. When Ernest answered, she gave him the same spiel, ending with, "So, what can you tell me about Riverside?"

Ernest was less subtle. He gave no response at all, and the line went dead. Bingo again!

THIRTY-NINE

VIVIAN MAINTAINED THAT Beth Abraham still needed a backup plan for the vacant lot, in case Will's proposal fell through. In case, somehow, Will got caught for all his indiscretions. In case, somehow, the synagogue was willing to say no to him. So she had continued to meet with Bree, Vera and Joel at the South Side CDC's office, developing their proposal for the mixed-income housing project. She had neglected to tell Vera and Joel about Joseph's directive to stop.

This time, sitting in her car after the meeting, it occurred to her that she was in Raymond's neighborhood, though she did not know exactly where he lived. It had been more than a week since he quit, during which time Vivian had come up with twenty ideas about what to do and gone ahead with none of them, still unsure that she knew the difference between support and meddling. *Oh, what the hell. It's Pastoring 101, not rocket science.* She hesitated, then found his number on her phone.

"Raymond, hi, it's Vivian."

"Hi, Rabbi."

"I wanted you to know I was thinking of you," Vivian said. "And of Mac. I'm so sorry about everything."

"Uh-huh?"

"Can I come visit you today?" Vivian said, tightening the grip of her left hand on the steering wheel, surprising herself with her own spontaneous request. "I know I may have only met him in passing once, but given what he's gone through, what you have gone through...I thought...I mean, only if you wanted."

"That's nice of you, Rabbi Vivian." Then a long silence.

Too long, maybe? Vivian wondered if the call was still active. Just as she was about to check, he spoke.

"You can come."

Did he want to see her? It seemed like the right thing, to visit in a time of need, of loss. Maybe even bring over some food. Her face got warm and red, and she could not lift her hand from the steering wheel, aware that *she* seemed to be the one in need of something, vulnerable to a force that felt a lot like shame.

· · ·

Vivian arrived on Phillips Lane holding a cake from the nearest grocery store. She had circled the block a few times to find

a parking spot. Though she was only just familiarizing herself with the South Side neighborhood, as she walked toward
Raymond's house, she convinced herself that she felt perfectly
comfortable.

"Hi, Rabbi," Raymond greeted her, standing behind a half-
opened door.

"Hi Raymond. Here, I brought you some cake," Vivian said,
handing him the box. Raymond opened the door the rest of the
way and accepted the offering with a half-smile. He walked into
a large space, the combined living-dining room, and placed the
cake on the table.

Standing there, Vivian studied the photographs, on the
walls, on the shelves. She wanted to ask Raymond about the
people in them. She noticed an old portrait of, she assumed,
Raymond and three siblings dressed in their Sunday best, his
parents standing tall and straight with their hands on the children's shoulders. Surrounding it were a variety of smaller snap-
shots of Mac at different ages, smiling in a Batman costume,
driving a go-kart, kissing his mom on the cheek.

Not knowing exactly what small talk would fit the situation,
all Vivian could think to do was jump to the heart of the matter.
"I'm so sorry, Raymond. I know there has been a big, um, rupture, and maybe it's not possible to heal it. But I wanted you to
know that I'm here, I'm on your...." She hesitated. "I'm here."

"It was time for me to go anyway, after so many years of...
well, it was just time to go." Raymond picked at the tape on the
side of the cake box. "I've talked to some buddies about other
places I can work closer to home, and I wouldn't have to work
nights. It's time for a change."

"But if we—"

"Look, I appreciate you coming all this way, Rabbi Vivian," Raymond interrupted. "But we both know I've never been an equal. I can tell you feel guilty about it, but that doesn't change anything."

Vivian was fidgeting with one of the pictures on the shelf atop the fireplace. In it, Raymond's hand was on Sheila's pregnant belly. His mouth was stretched into a grin, but Vivian thought she could see pre-parenting fear in his eyes. "I understand. I also wanted you to know that I know you didn't do it, and that so many other—"

Raymond coughed. Or laughed. Vivian could not tell. He grabbed onto the chair from the dining room set and looked Vivian straight in the eye, as if daring her to finish putting both feet in her mouth. She opened her mouth once but nothing came out.

"Well, I'm very sorry, again," she continued, finally finding the words. "I know that's not going to change anything, either." Vivian clenched her fists as if squeezing invisible stress balls. "And if you, or Mac or anyone, still want a rabbi from the synagogue to sign onto a letter about police funding or show up to a protest or something, I'll do it. I'll get Harry and the board to agree."

"Thank you, Rabbi."

Vivian wanted to offer him a hug before leaving, but there was too much distance. She nodded and turned toward the door.

"Rabbi, wait," Raymond said. "Today, the company you all bought the new oven from called to reschedule the installation. They had my cell number. I told them I don't work at the synagogue anymore, and they should follow up with who-ever else they had on file." Raymond looked down at his folded hands.

"The guy on the phone said he had already tried to call Jeffrey, and when I asked who that was, he said, 'You know, the one who originally postponed the delivery.' As in, *before* the fire. Seemed like a clue, or something."

Vivian smiled awkwardly and nodded with gratitude. Walk-ing toward her car, she tried mentally composing a list of Jef-freys. But she was too distracted, instead replaying the whole conversation in her head, all her incomplete babbling. What had she been trying to accomplish with this visit? Did she accomplish any of it?

Looking up, she noticed a group of young men walking in her direction, carrying campaign signs and joking around. One looked like Alex Santiago, and as the group got closer, Vivian also made out the face she had just seen in Raymond's pictures, Mac Weeks. They approached each other and Vivian wondered if she should say anything.

They finally met on a stretch of sidewalk made narrow by the obstruction of a large Japanese maple tree. The group low-ered their volume and crowded to one side, walking more slowly and letting Vivian pass. She offered a quiet greeting, consider-ing all the things she could not bring herself to say. Mac stared, as if trying to place her. Alex handed her a button as she walked past: *Santiago for Mayor*. The "o" in Santiago was in the shape of a raised fist.

"Vote for me," he said.

"And ease your guilt about displacing Black folks," another

voice said. Vivian smiled awkwardly and looked down at the ground. Mac, who was at the end of the line, dramatically bowed his head and stretched out his arms out into the direction Vivian was walking, signaling her to proceed first. She did. A few feet past them, Vivian turned around briefly, and she saw Mac glancing back, too.

As she drove toward her neighborhood on the other side of the city, she swung from thought to thought: if Mac knew who she was and could feel her empathy in their brief encounter, whether or not Raymond would take her up on her offer, and how the hell Will Gould, and some guy named Jeffrey, started the fire.

FORTY

THE SKY WAS caught somewhere between day and dusk as Vivian neared home. She loved this time of evening, when there was no more work to do, when she could cook herself some dinner, call an old friend, or get lost in a Rabbi Small mystery novel.

Her phone buzzed. It was a text from Lisa. *Finally talked to Carrie & co. about renting BA our space. We're in! Let's talk details soon.* A smile spread across Vivian's face. Maybe it wouldn't lead to the deep interfaith partnership with First Parish that she dreamed of, but it was something. She would take whatever wins she could get.

Arriving home, she propped open the door with one leg to

let in light from the hallway, maneuvering some grocery bags out of her arms and onto the floor.

"Hello, Vivian," a deep voice said.

Vivian shrieked and dropped her bags. She quickly flipped the light switch. Will Gould was sitting on her couch, his feet resting on the coffee table.

"Aren't you one for drama," Will said, picking up a tomato that had rolled toward his feet.

"You're the one who broke into my house! What the hell are you doing here?" Vivian could feel her own swallowing in her ears. She tried to remember anything at all from the self-defense class she took in college.

"Listen, Viv," Will said, standing up. "Stop snooping around. You're under contract to sing some songs, go to a rally for some environmental cause, and maybe attract young faces to the synagogue. Don't mess with the way things are."

Vivian calculated her response. She thought of all the mystery novels she had read, which universally suggested that a suspect threatening the detective, late at night, in a compromised position, did not bode well. But this was reality, and Will probably didn't do his own dirty work anyway. He was here just to scare her. Right?

"But you get to mess with things however you please?" she asked, surprised by her own chutzpah.

"That's how it works," Will said, stretching out his hands, as though saying he did not write the rules. "This deal will go through, and it'll be good for everyone. Stop trying to derail a good thing."

"You can't treat people like this." Vivian's voice cracked as she realized, mid-sentence, that this line of attack would go nowhere with Will Gould. She did not have all the pieces figured out, or any real proof for that matter. But she knew that Will was up to no good, and that he was worried about it. Why else would he be standing in front of her, in her home? He was posturing intimidation, but his very presence conveyed weakness.

She took a gamble. "I know that the math on Riverside's contracts doesn't all add up."

"You don't know what the hell you're talking about, Viv." He kept calling her that. *Viv*. She hated it. "And you certainly can't talk to me like this. Keep it up and I'll destroy you."

"You can't break into my house, but here you are."

"I can do whatever the hell I want," Will said.

"You can't get away with this, Will. The scams, the…." Vivian did not finish her thought. She had already crossed the line.

"The what?" Will said.

Vivian was silent. He yelled and kicked the leg of the coffee table. "The what?"

"The fire," she said, as if the words willed themselves out of her mouth. She looked him straight in the eyes until he turned away, laughing heartily.

"Now you're in a real hysteria, Viv."

Will's voice got stern as he continued. "Burn down a synagogue I donated money to build? Does that make sense? Have you never heard of antisemites? No one would ever believe you."

"We'll see about that," Vivian said, trying to sound strong, not quite sure if she did.

Will walked over to her, stomping loudly on a stray bag of pita chips, and stopped a few inches away. Vivian tensed up as he towered over her in her home that suddenly felt so small and lonely.

"You just wait and see how all the chips fall. You're done, *Viv*." He bent down so his eyes were staring straight into hers. He snapped his fingers. "Just like that."

"Get out of my house," she said, in the same unconvincing tone, trying to hide her fear.

He walked out, slamming the door so hard that the mezuzah fell off the doorpost.

Vivian could not move. Once she heard the front door of the apartment building slam, she opened her door to retrieve it. She held the mezuzah tightly and brought it back inside, laying it gently on the coffee table.

Vivian sat in her armchair. The couch now seemed tainted. She stared at her mezuzah, adorned with metal flowers. It seemed just as vulnerable as her. She thought of the last time she was this shaken. The night of the fire. And then she remembered falling asleep in Karla's arms. But it was dark and she and Karla were…maybe…done? *Done*, she thought. *You're done*, Will's words, echoed in her ears. What *would* Will Gould do?

FORTY-ONE

V IVIAN HAD TWISTED and turned in her bed that night, replaying the events of the last few days and weeks. Minutes after eight a.m., her cell phone rang, startling her awake. It was Joseph, who always expected her to answer right away. There could have been a death in the community, or something else just as urgent. But she needed to get her bearings first. She let the phone ring and sprawled in bed, preparing for the day.

"*Modeh ani l'fanecha*. I thank you, God, for returning my soul to me," she whispered to herself, unexpectedly. She had said this prayer every morning as a child, but it had not been a part of her routine for years.

Vivian arose from the comfort of her floral duvet cover, brushed her teeth, put on her work clothes and called back.

Joseph did not bother with pleasantries when he picked up. "Are you sabotaging the deal with Will? Are you still working with another developer?"

It had not been even 24 hours, and Will was already working his channels against her. "I wouldn't put it like that. We need to have options, Joseph. I know some people in the city who are looking for a place to build mixed-income housing, and it seemed prudent to talk with them."

"You cannot be doing that. I told you to stop it." This was the angriest she had ever heard Joseph. His tone reminded Vivian of her father's, chastising her for her few experiments with angsty teenage rebellion.

She paced across her apartment, weaving between the bedroom and living room. "And why not? We haven't signed any contract, and it's good to have backup plans if anything goes wrong."

"The only contract you should be worried about here is your own. This is Will's deal, and we need him. We need him to get through the renovation process and we need to keep him as an important member of our community."

"Joseph, we have to—"

"I'd be careful if I were you," Joseph interrupted. "You are on very thin ice here, Vivian. Will wants you gone. I'm trying to vouch for you here, but if you keep fighting back, I'll have no choice."

"That's bullshit, Joseph."

"Excuse me?"

She stopped pacing, planting her feet firmly on the ground in front of a photograph of her mother and two grandmothers, smiling widely at Vivian's bat mitzvah. "You *do* have a choice here. You're choosing Will over me. You're choosing money over…." Vivian let out a breath. "There's more at stake here, Joseph."

"What are you talking about?"

Vivian had wanted to wait until she figured out the whole chain of events before making any public declaration. But she was stuck, and all these men were backing her into a corner. "Will started the fire."

"What?" Joseph said, in an uncharacteristically high voice. "That's ridiculous."

"It's the truth."

"He wasn't even in the country, Vivian. What—"

"When Will Gould wants to make something happen, he makes it happen, physical whereabouts be damned."

"Vivian, please, this is…I can't even recognize you right now."

Because I'm fighting back? she thought.

"How…why on earth would he do that?" Joseph asked.

"I…um…I don't know that just yet," Vivian said, falling backward into her yellow sofa.

"Are you serious?" Joseph said. "You're accusing our biggest donor, one of the most influential people in this city, and you have no evidence? And you only bring this up when your job is on the line?"

"It's not like I'm calling a press conference about it, Joseph. You're the one threatening me here. Don't turn this around. We all know Will Gould is not a man of deep integrity. You just tell yourself the story that he is, so you can ignore the fact that you bow at his feet anyway." She paused. "Like an idol."

The line was silent. "Vivian, what you are doing here is dangerous," Joseph finally said, burying Vivian's insult. "What do you want? To turn our synagogue upside down?"

She stood up. "Look around, Joseph. It's already upside down."

"We need this deal," Joseph said. Vivian could hear him pacing, too, to calm himself down. "We need Will. Please, I want you to be able to stay, but—"

"Then fight for me to stay," Vivian said.

"You've got to let this go and apologize to Will, and let things go back to—let things, uh, settle down."

Now it was her turn to be silent, to let the tension between them remain palpable. Without hearing any more from Joseph, Vivian hung up.

FORTY-TWO

V IVIAN SLOWLY SETTLED into her car, preparing to drive
across the city again to hammer out more of the proposal
with Bree, Vera and Joel. She sat still, staring at a magnolia tree
across the street. It had been so beautiful the week before. Now
the flowers were brown, and most of their petals lay on the sidewalk, trampled into a gooey mess by pedestrians.

Who could she call? Who would help Vivian think through
this bind? Her mom would get too worried. Heather and Lisa
were too close to it all. And Karla was not an option anymore.
Mimi!

Mimi was Vivian's rabbi in college, the one who had inspired
Vivian to walk the path she was now on, who showed her how

to add her own voice to the cross-generational conversation of rabbinic sages when making a complex discernment. They had learned together each week back then, struggling with the text, with each other. Through their study, Vivian learned to love the tug of war between obedience and critique, the ideal and the real.

Vivian held fast to Mimi as a mentor while she explored her own rabbinic path, even as Mimi moved on to her own congregation in Wisconsin. Mimi was the one she called before saying yes to the offer from Beth Abraham. Mimi's was the voice that argued with other rabbis in Vivian's head as she developed sermons and classes, reminding her to grapple with the challenges of the here and the now.

What would Rabbi Mimi do, her mentor, her friend? How would she make sense of the conundrum in which Vivian found herself?

She picked up after a few rings. "Vivian?"

"Mimi!" Vivian said, her shoulders loosening automatically. "How are you? How's Milwaukee?"

"Good," Mimi said, chewing loudly into the receiver. "Just preparing my sermon for Shavuot. To what do I owe this pleasure of a midday call?"

"There is so much to say," Vivian said, leaning forward over the steering wheel. She explained her predicament: the fire, the lack of proof, Will's threat, the various plans for the vacant land, Joseph's ultimatum. "What do I do?"

Vivian could almost see her mentor's distinctive thinking face: tapping her mouth with two curved fingers, head tilted up as though something curious was happening on the ceiling above her. "I've been fixating on a midrash you and I learned once," Mimi said, "the one about how the Israelites did not initially consent to receiving the Torah. Instead, they were forced to, when God pressured them by dangling Mount Sinai over their heads. But because contracts made under duress are not actually valid under Jewish law, our ancestors had to *re*-accept the Torah later."

When Mimi and Vivian had studied this text together years before, Vivian had understood, even sympathized with, God's harshness. The Israelites were so broken, they could not have built communal consensus. They needed something that united them, and God had provided it. Mimi, on the other hand, had not let God off the hook.

"Sounds like Joseph is holding the mountain over your head," Mimi continued, "and acting as though you're getting something out of it. And this Will character, I'm not too sure he wouldn't just drop the whole thing on you."

"Me, and all of Beth Abraham."

"Someone's got to challenge these guys," Mimi said. "Keep digging. You, and the rest of the community, deserve some choice in the matter."

"Thank you. I needed to hear that," Vivian said.

"Aha! I knew I'd pull you over to my side eventually."

Vivian howled with laughter as she hung up. Her eyes caught on a magnolia flower atop the tree, one that was still in bloom. She breathed in deeply, as if she could smell that one's freshness over the surrounding rot, and drove south.

. . .

Leaning over the blueprints laid out on the drawing table at Bree's office, Vivian continued to defy Joseph's orders. Bree walked the group through one of the possible layouts, sharing the measurements, plans for the grounds and communal space, the distribution of units for families and seniors, the infrastructure available so that seniors could age in place.

Joel traced one of the units with his finger. Vera asked questions about the affordable housing lottery and the mechanisms it would use to determine the building's residents. Bree had an answer for every question. She described the potential tax breaks (including a big one they could qualify for if Margaret Heath won—and fulfilled her campaign promises), and the plans to categorize parts of the project differently, so that the senior units would not be subject to the lottery. Vivian was mostly quiet. And they were all very impressed. It would be a long shot, but the subcommittee was ready to bring their plan to the board.

Vivian lingered after Vera and Joel left, chatting with Bree.

"You were uncharacteristically quiet in that meeting," Bree said. "What's going on?"

Vivian told her about the call with Joseph. There was far more to the story that she could not share, but Bree had no trouble imagining a development deal alone as grounds for the kind of interference Will was running.

"Why do these men always hold the mountain over our heads?" Vivian said.

Bree looked up from re-rolling the blueprints, puzzled. Vivian recounted the midrash that she and Mimi had discussed earlier.

"It's a bit dramatic, but that sounds about right," Bree said, now shimmying the blueprints back into their cardboard tube.

"But what if," she continued, "as God was dangling the mountain above their heads, some people raised up their arms to hold it? To take it from God, or hold the weight together, or something?"

Vivian took a deep breath, releasing a bit more of the tension that now seemed permanently lodged in her shoulders. She closed her eyes and shifted her focus to the faces of the people at the bottom of Mount Sinai, supporting its weight, even lifting it up. She imagined Vera, Joel, Bree, Mimi, and the rest of her congregation, all there with her, struggling together.

"That's beautiful, Bree," she said. "Mind if I quote you in my sermon tomorrow?"

FORTY-THREE

I F VIVIAN WAS GOING to get fired for picking a fight with
Will Gould, she figured that she might as well challenge her
community in the process. She had gone over and over what
she would say in her sermon, how she would soften the midrash she could not shake, shift its light and focus on what was in
the hearts and minds of the people underneath the mountain.
She would add her voice—to Mimi's, to Bree's. A new midrashic
tradition.

On the morning of Shavuot, Vivian walked up to the makeshift bima, which was a stage with a music stand at the East Side
Community Center, to make her offering. Will, who barely ever
came to services, was in the second row of folding chairs, and

Vivian could feel his gaze on her. Joseph's and Harry's, too. She straightened her back, tightened her jaw and began to speak.

"When our ancestors were standing at Mount Sinai on the day of Shavuot, about to accept the Torah, our Rabbis tell us that God dangled the mountain over their heads. They were forced to accept the holy doctrine—or face death. The midrash continues on to say that because the commitment happened under duress, this contract, between God and the Israelites, was actually invalid. And so, we had to actively accept the Torah, our inheritance, once more, at a separate juncture.

"This is a troubling text. And yet, inside of it lives a glimmer of our collective free will. The possibility that we, as a people, get to define the terms of our commitments. When I shared this teaching with a friend recently, she offered a beautiful midrash-on-the-midrash that shifts the spotlight. 'What if a few of the Israelites standing under the mountain,' she said, 'put up their arms to hold it?'

"That image has stuck with me. What if others then followed their brave example, until *everyone* was holding up the hovering mountain, together? What if our ancestors—and our own spirits, because the rabbis tell us that the soul of every Jew throughout history was present that day—what if they accepted the Torah only in *partnership* with God? What if the Torah itself is a symbol, the very foundation, of shared power?"

Vivian let the question linger as she observed the strange scene. The rows full of congregants in metal folding chairs, the basketball hoops looming above their heads. Even the sound of silence was different here.

"As we rebuild from the fire, there will be many decisions

to make as a community. We can choose to hold the mountain up together."

From behind her on the stage, Vivian could hear Joseph's metal chair creak. In front of her, Harry's chair echoed the sound as Vivian watched him shift positions. She noticed two unexpected faces just behind Harry: Ben and Flora. For a moment, she stared at them, and memories from the night of the fire flooded her brain.

"We have gone through a lot as a community over the past several weeks," Vivian said, pushing herself to continue, both distracted and buoyed by her discovery. "Our synagogue, our refuge, has been irreparably damaged. We are here in this strange place that does not feel much like home. We are scared. The echoes of the antisemitic threats we face are resounding. But we are finding a way forward, too. We are davening in this community center open to all. I am working from the office of the church down the street from Beth Abraham, which has also offered space for future services. So many people and leaders in Providence have supported us in this time, offering pathways to partnership. They have joined us at the foot of the mountain, bearing some of its weight.

"We have an opportunity to return the favor. To reach out our hands to our neighbors, help hold up what is bearing down on them. We can be so much stronger when we pull together, when we overcome our fear and see each other in our foundation, when we envision that we, along with our whole community, were standing together at Sinai holding up the mountain.

"So. What vision of Torah do we accept today? And who do we envision at the foot of the mountain receiving it?" She swept the auditorium with her gaze, surveying her flock, until suddenly, she found her eyes locked with...Karla's. She was standing at the back of the room.

Vivian cleared her throat as she fought another battle in the losing war to stay focused, dearly hoping there would be no more audience surprises. "We will soon decide as a congregation what to do with our vacant property, a plot of land that has remained empty—but full of potential—for years. In that same amount of time, families who have lived in Providence for decades have been, and continue to be, displaced as a result of rising housing and land prices.

"The fire destroyed so much of our communal home. And yet, it has given us an opportunity to sharpen our focus—about who we want to be, what commitments we will make, and who we even include in our *we*. I urge us, as we begin to answer these questions, to envision the widest possible collective holding the weight of our shared burdens. I wish us all a meaningful holiday."

. . .

"I warned you," Will said, rushing over to Vivian in the front corner of the auditorium after the service ended. "And don't think this won't follow you outside Providence." Without giving her a chance to respond, he ran off—in search of Joseph, Vivian assumed.

A few more congregants lined up to comment on her sermon. Some thanked her. Sally Schwartz-Kaplan and Farah Rice walked over to ask more about the possible options for the vacant lot. As Vera explained the ins and outs of the affordable housing lottery, Shlomo Seidel interrupted them. He chastised Vivian for ignoring the needs of their Jewish community while Farah and Sally looked on, taken aback.

"Excuse me, sir. I'd like to talk with the rabbi," said another voice. It was Karla, cutting her way through the crowd. Her words disrupted Shlomo's rant and he left in a huff, followed by Sally and Farah, who nodded gratefully at this mysterious newcomer.

Vivian stood up straight and tried to compose herself.

"Are you lost? You know this is a synagogue service, right?" Vivian wasn't sure, herself, if she was joking or expressing the anger she still held.

"Your sermon was beautiful," Karla said. "That image, all of us holding up the mountain together. I love that."

"What are you doing here?" Vivian asked.

"I needed to talk to you, and I knew this is where you'd be. And I knew you'd have to respond civilly in front of all your congregants."

"If only Will had the same self-restraint," Vivian whispered, guessing Karla had seen their interaction. By this time most people had trickled out, including, to Vivian's dismay, Flora and Ben. There were only a few congregants left to greet.

"Wait here for a few minutes and we can talk privately," she said. As she turned away from Karla, she added, "And don't worry. Even with no one around, I'll try to stay civil."

. . .

"There's so much to say," Karla began, as they walked together in a nearby park. The path was lined with oak trees that glowed in the midday sun. "I was looking through some files the other day. It turns out that when Mike took over as mayor for a few months, he authorized a construction permit for Riverside Developers to build condos on your synagogue's land." They both took a few more synchronized steps. "The date it was signed was in March."

"But nothing's been officially decided," Vivian said, turning toward Karla. "You heard."

"I figured. That's why I came by now."

"To incriminate your boss?"

"To hold up the mountain with you," Karla said. "I found a few more premature permits in his files, when I was, you know...."

"Snooping?"

"I was innocently cleaning out his desk, just like a compliant female underling, and stumbled upon them." Karla curtsied theatrically. "And there's more. Gould's campaign check bounced. I asked a friend at City Hall for some intel, and she said there have been several complaints lately...contractors and vendors that Riverside hasn't paid. A bunch of their project deadlines have been delayed, to boot."

"Seems like Will's trying to close deals before people find out the money's not there," Vivian said, as she watched a group of teenagers playing frisbee. One of them leapt into the air, extending her whole arm, to make a beautiful grab.

"After your text," Vivian continued, "I did some research of my own. Riverside's been in hot water a few times, but in each case, nothing happened. The investigations magically disappeared—in the press, with the city." She paused. "And then, a few nights ago, I came back to my apartment and Will was just sitting there, threatening me to stop my own snooping."

"*What?*" Karla said, halting her steps and reaching for Vivian's forearm. "That happened for real? You didn't mix that up with one of your mystery novels?"

"He was just sitting on my couch, like it was totally normal to break into my house."

"Are you okay?"

"I'm fine," Vivian said, reaching toward a lush tree branch that leaned onto their path. "It was definitely more dramatic than most of my interactions with powerful men, but something about it felt eerily familiar."

"Vivian, I think—"

"I know, Karla."

"Will started the fire!" they said, simultaneously.

"How did you know?" Karla asked.

"A few clues turned up here and there. And Will's threat sealed the deal," Vivian said. "Also, when I accused him—"

"You *what*?!"

"Well, he caught me off guard. It was all kind of surreal and the accusation just came out. Anyway, he got defensive, and he was already in my fucking apartment in the dark."

Vivian caught sight of a labradoodle running toward her, pulling its owner along. The dog sniffed her shoes. Vivian bent down to pet it, and she asked the scripted questions about its name and age. Its name was Mo, short for Moses. On Shavuot, of all days. Vivian could not help but take that as a sign. Of what, she did not know.

"I have an idea," Karla said, a trace of mischief in her tone.

They had returned to the beginning of the path's loop and kept walking. "I think I should leak the story about the permits to the press. It wouldn't focus solely on the Riverside project, since there were a few others. Even if it won't stop Will's acquisition of your land, it will slow down the process and make things sticky for him."

"You're willing to make your boss look bad, maybe even throw the campaign, for this? For me?"

"I guess so," Karla said, smirking.

"Thank you," Vivian said, stopping. Karla stopped too. Vivian abruptly leaned over to hug her.

"There's a lot here that still doesn't add up," she said, with her chin still resting on Karla's shoulder. "Will was on vacation that night."

"Right. I remember that detail," Karla said, pulling back. "Do you know Jay Rosenfeld?"

"Jay...Jay," Vivian said, trying to will a eureka moment into existence. "I know a Jeffrey Rosenfeld. He's a member of the synagogue, doesn't come very much."

"Yeah, same guy. He goes by Jay. Anyway, he works for Will. He's his money guy and all-around right-hand man."

"Wait," Vivian said, extending both arms toward Karla in a "stop right there" motion. "Are you sure? I mean, there could easily be a handful of Jeff and Josh and Jay Rosenfelds in this town."

"It's the same guy. I'm sure of it," Karla said. "He was at the synagogue the day of the press conference, whispering to Will. And he seemed quite friendly with your boss. I've never seen Will without Jay by his side."

Vivian's eyes grew wide. "Raymond just told me that somebody named Jeffrey postponed the oven installation, and—"

"Whoa, whoa, whoa," Karla interrupted. "Slow down."

Vivian pulled Karla off the path under a shady tree. She did a quick swivel to check for any familiar faces. There were only the frisbee players and some more dog walkers, definitely not wearing their holiday best.

"Do you think," Vivian whispered, "that Will got Jeffrey— Jay—to start the fire?"

"Guys like Will don't cut their own meat," Karla said. "It seems pretty plausible they wouldn't start their own fires."

"I think we need to buy ourselves some time to put this puzzle together."

"It's settled, then," Karla said, clasping her hands together. "I'm going to leak the story."

"Leak it in the *Herald*, not the *Chronicle*," Vivian suggested. "They wouldn't publish anything harmful about Gould."

"Someone's gotten savvy," Karla said, raising an eyebrow. They returned to the path and continued their walk in comfortable silence.

"I'm sorry about the press coverage that day," Karla said eventually. "I got swept up in it all."

"I'm sorry about how I reacted," Vivian said, a few paces later. "I know things are more complicated than they seem."

Karla squeezed Vivian's hand. "Thank you."

"Can we pick up where we left off?" Vivian said, reciprocating. "You know, before I walked out on you and your enchiladas?"

Karla stopped walking and put her arms around Vivian. "We

do make a pretty good team," she said. A light breeze gusted through the trees and blew wisps of hair onto Vivian's cheeks. Karla brushed them to the side and kissed her.

FORTY-FOUR

THE NEXT DAY, Vivian had no time to worry about losing her job. Karla was back in the picture and Vivian had a crime to solve.

She started by calling R & J Appliances. She told the clerk, Oscar, that she would be taking over coordination of the oven installation since Raymond no longer worked for Beth Abraham, and she asked to be brought up to date with a summary of communication about the order.

Vivian could hear him shuffling papers in the background. As he reviewed the file, Oscar read aloud.

"March 24th: Initial inquiry about high-capacity ovens. By phone, caller Raymond Weeks, client Beth Abraham.

"April 9th: Order placed, delivery scheduled for May 16th. By phone, Raymond Weeks again.

"May 16th: Delivery postponed."

The day of the fire! Vivian thought. She could hear Oscar breathing as he kept reading.

"And that was a phone call from…ah, it's tough to make out the name. Some of these guys have got such shitty handwriting. It's not Raymond, though. Maybe Jacky, Jeremy?"

"Could it be Jeffrey?" Vivian asked.

"There we go," Oscar said. "Jeffrey…Riverside, it looks like. Must've taken over from the Raymond guy before you got there."

Vivian instinctively raised her arms, gesturing a touchdown like a football referee. She was dimly aware of Oscar mentioning, as an aside, that day-of cancellations were a royal pain in R & J's collective ass. She let him know that the delay would unfortunately be extended for a while, as other renovations were now necessary before a new oven could be installed. She thanked him and said goodbye.

"Wait," Oscar said. "That last note says Jeffrey added a bunch of stuff to the order. Fourteen each of a bunch of appliances, for condo units at the same address. Are those on hold now too?"

"Thank you, Oscar. You've been very helpful," Vivian said. Leaving his question unanswered, she tapped 'Stop Recording' on her phone screen.

FORTY-FIVE

THE SECOND PAGE of the *Providence Herald* carried the story, under the headline, "McCann Issues Dirty Permits to Developers." Karla had anonymously left an envelope of photocopied documents in the mailbox of one of the editors she knew.

McCann was despondent at all of his campaign events following the article's release. Reporters and constituents persisted in asking him about it. He tried to redirect to his plans for smart growth, but inevitably the question would get asked again, and his dodges made less and less sense. He was quickly losing whatever edge he had.

Margaret Heath capitalized on McCann's blunders. Rather

than directly reference the controversy, she focused on her plans to hold developers accountable to higher property taxes and ensure that project contracts accounted for broader communal needs, like affordable housing and green space.

When news broke that the developers who had exploited their power with city officials were also behind an onslaught of negative TV ads against Heath, she used it to her advantage. Her campaign painted her as a bulwark against corruption. Her staff packed her calendar with community groups who had initially endorsed McCann; they were all wavering.

Karla did her best to get through each day, knowing it would be a slog to the end. She began taking more breaks, sometimes sneaking out to see Vivian. That was how Karla found herself parked with Vivian in front of a sprawling Victorian home on Providence's eastern edge.

. . .

Vivian's hand lingered on the passenger door handle as she stared out the window.

"Look at me," Karla said, and she turned to face the driver's seat. "You can do this, Vivian. You've already stood up to Will freaking Gould."

"But what if everything blows up in my face?" she asked, leaning back against her seat.

"You've already made it pretty clear that you are willing to risk that. And you're not alone." Karla rested her right fingers on Vivian's leg. "Just take a few deep breaths. I know you can do this."

She squeezed Karla's hand and left the car. She walked up to the door, held her fist in midair and knocked. A balding man around the same height as Vivian, with large glasses and a wrinkled shirt, opened it.

"Rabbi Vivian," Jay Rosenfeld gulped, not bothering to smile. "What are you doing here? No one's sitting shiva or anything."

Vivian had strategized with Karla about her approach. No pleasantries, they decided. She had to convey confidence, regardless of how she felt.

"We have some business to discuss, Jay."

"And what's that?" he asked, putting up his hand against the doorpost.

Vivian was having trouble getting a good read on his body language. "How come you delayed the order for the synagogue's new oven?"

Jay's jaw stiffened. "With all due respect," he said, "I don't need to answer your questions, Vivian. I've got a lot of other *actual* business to attend to."

Cleaning up the mess from the *Herald* article, Vivian figured. She felt powerful for an instant, knowing she had a hand in the frustrations of this man so proximate to power. She adjusted her posture again. "This is important."

"Fine," Jay surrendered. "I've been helping Harry out with some of the synagogue logistics. He's got a lot on his plate."

"Sounds like you've got a lot on your plate, too," Vivian said. "Why would you get involved in something as small as that?"

Jay's lips thinned. "I've already answered your unimportant question. I've got to go. My son has a Little League game." He tried to shut the door, but Vivian caught it, surprised at her own chutzpah.

"Not so fast," she said. She pushed the door back toward him, revealing a foyer strewn with the messy trappings of children's baseball. Behind it, Vivian saw the kitchen, where a tower of dirty dishes tottered in the sink.

"You were at Beth Abraham the night of the fire," Vivian said. "Right?"

"A lot of people were there." Jay's voice broke.

"Jay," Vivian said, riding the momentum of the moment. There was no turning back now. "Did you start the fire?"

"We're done here," he said, and slammed the door closed.

Vivian's heart was pounding like it did after a Zumba class. He was definitely guilty. The evasion, the posturing, the cracks in his tough-guy facade. She took an envelope from her tote bag, crouched down and slipped it under the front door. In it was the transcript of her call with R & J, the date of Jay's call circled in red pen. Vivian knew it was not bulletproof evidence, but it was a lead. Add Riverside's financial woes and Will's threats to the equation, and the whole picture started to come into focus.

Vivian stayed in a crouch, ear to Jay's door, listening for movement. She could not discern any identifiable sounds. She rose and walked swiftly back toward Karla, who had parked a few houses away to avoid Jay's line of sight.

Vivian opened the car door and angled her way in. "He did it. I'm sure of it," she said, looking straight ahead through the windshield.

Karla leaned in. "Did he confess?"

Vivian turned toward her. "Not with his words. But definitely with everything else."

"So, let me get this straight. You just got a confession from Will Gould's fall guy?"

"If you think body language counts as a confession."

"That's pretty hot," Karla said, raising one eyebrow.

Vivian smiled. "There's no time for that, Karla."

"Time for what? Flirting?" She pulled Vivian toward her. "Making out?"

Karla leaned in and initiated a kiss. Vivian got into it for a few blissful moments, then she pulled back and put her hands on Karla's shoulders.

"Back to the issue at hand. What do we do now? The pieces are starting to fall into place. But even with the article, Will still has everyone wrapped around his finger. There's no way Jay goes public with this. Will can probably just stop the investigation in its tracks.

"In the Rabbi Small mysteries," Vivian continued, "the reveal always happens so neatly. He figures it out, and then, bam, the person is caught. And that's it. But this is a total mess."

"Are they moving forward on firing you?" Karla asked.

"There's a board meeting tomorrow night to finalize a plan for the land," Vivian said. "And despite the permit scandal, I know that most of the board members, and Joseph too, still want the Riverside deal. From what I hear, Will is planning to grace that meeting with his royal presence and propose that they get rid of me."

Karla stroked her chin. "Maybe you should make an unexpected visit to a guilty man two days in a row."

"You mean, go to the meeting?"

Karla nodded.

"And say what?" Vivian said, raising her voice. "Call Will out?"

"Make him lie in front of everyone," Karla said. "What do you have to lose at this point if he's after you?"

"That just sounds so, so—"

"Brilliant? Bold? Badass?" Karla filled in the blanks.

"So much like something Will Gould would do." Vivian rolled the idea around in her head. She laughed.

"Man, we go on some strange dates," she said, rubbing Karla's leg. "Let's get some dinner, I'm exhausted."

"You got it, babe," Karla said, driving off.

FORTY-SIX

"**L**ET'S GET RIGHT to it," Will said, surrounded by the executive members of Beth Abraham's board, who found themselves once again in Harry's living room. "Rabbi Vivian has been plotting against me and the broader interests of the community for a while now. I strongly suggest that she be fired."

"That sermon was uncalled for," Harry agreed, backing Will up.

"Let's not jump to conclusions here. She brings so much to this community," Vera said.

"Perhaps I wasn't clear. This isn't negotiable, Vera. Either she goes, or I pull my offer. And my membership," Will said.

"Whoa, whoa, whoa. Let's all calm down," Harry said, surprised, as if Will had gone off script. "Will, we know it's been a hard week. We still want to make the deal work."

Vera let out a questioning grunt.

"So, let's hammer it out," Shlomo said, reaching for the yet-untouched crackers and cheese that Harry had laid out on the coffee table.

"Not until that bitch is gone," Will said, through clenched jaws.

"Excuse me?" Joseph said. "Will, you can't—uh, I'd appreciate it if you didn't use that language. Let's have a calm conversation about this. We are fighting so many battles: against antisemitism, the fire. Let's not add this, okay? You heard Harry, we want the deal to work."

"She's stoking the flames here," Will said. "Firing her will give us a fresh start," he added, in a calmer tone.

Will's words hung in the air. The doorbell rang and echoed through the room. Everyone sighed in relief as Harry went to answer.

. . .

A moment later, Vivian marched into the living room. Vera and Shlomo, who were both using the break to refill their snack plates, froze. Harry ran in behind Vivian.

"You can't just—" he huffed.

"What the hell are you doing here?" Will interrupted, eyes bulging.

Vivian planted her feet firmly at the entrance of the room.

Nothing Will could do would make her stumble. "If you're going to fire me," Vivian said, "at least let me have a say."

Will shot a menacing look Harry's way.

"Uh, Vivian. Rabbi Vivian. You were not invited to this meeting." Harry's voice shook.

"Well, I'm staying," she said.

"See? How can you put up with this, this uppity behavior?" Will said.

"*Uppity?*" Vera said. "I draw my line there. I say we give Vivian a chance to defend herself, tell her side of the story."

Bolstered by Vera, Vivian took the opening. "Will, before we sign on the dotted line, I think it's important that everyone here knows what you've done."

"We saw the paper, Vivian. There's no need to rub his nose in it," Joseph said quietly.

"That's not what I'm talking about, Joseph," Vivian said. "Will, you had your chance to come clean privately. And you didn't. So here we are."

Meetings were never fun, but from the minimal eye contact and matching crossed arms of everyone present, it was clear that this was indeed the least fun board meeting any of them had ever attended.

"Will started the fire," Vivian said.

"Vivian!" Joseph gasped.

"That is ridiculous." Will laughed. "I was out of the country on business. How could I have done that? It was antisemites. Now seriously, everyone. You can see that it's time for her to go." Will's eyes seemed angrier to Vivian as they settled on her.

"You got Jay Rosenfeld to do your dirty work."

"This is crazy!" Will stood up. "I do you all a favor coming to Beth Abraham," he continued, jabbing a finger into the air. "I'm the biggest donor. I put you on the map. I will not waste any more time and be subjected to *her* vilification. I could have sealed a deal for ten million instead of being here." He turned to Harry. "Call me when the meeting's over. I'm giving you the best offer you'll get. Don't any of you forget that."

Will gathered up his briefcase and suit jacket. He made his way out of the room, passing Harry in a leather armchair.

"Will, did you do it?" Harry whispered.

"Harry? *Harry*?!" Will said, bending down a little and gripping his friend's arms. "Are you really asking me that?"

"Answer the question," Harry said.

The doorbell rang again.

Harry waited for Will to say something, but he just gasped and stared.

"I'll be right back," Harry said, getting up.

He returned moments later, Jay Rosenfeld slouching behind him. The leather couches squeaked with their occupants' surprise. Vivian's feet felt stuck in their place.

Will's face reddened. "What the hell are *you* doing here?"

"The right thing," Jay said. Will's upper body began to tremble.

"Will, I asked you a question," Harry interrupted. "Were you responsible for the fire?"

"Of course not," Will answered, looking straight at Jay.

"He's lying," Jay cried. Shlomo choked on his cracker. "He made me do it," Jay continued. "He said he'd fire me if I didn't.

You have to understand, my family—we just bought a new house—prep school is so expensive—I didn't have a choice."

I didn't have a choice. Vivian repeated the words in her head. The same words that Joseph has used when he threatened to fire her if she kept meddling. *Of course, they have choices*, she thought.

"How could you?" Joseph asked, staring at Will.

Backed into a corner, Will rubbed his hands on the sides of his pants, recalibrating his strategy. "Come on. Why is everyone getting hysterical? No one was really injured, and I'm going to get you a great deal with the insurance money."

"So you admit it? You started the fire?" Harry said.

"No," Will snapped. "You heard. Jay started the fire."

Vivian spoke up. "Will, in the real world, when you make the call, you are most certainly responsible. And you face the consequences."

"We'll see about that," Will said, turning toward the door.

"You're sick, Will," Vera said.

"No, lady. I'm powerful. No one will ever take your word against mine," Will said, looking at Vivian.

"Well, what about mine?" Vera said. The tension was at its peak, as though it might shatter all of Harry's fragile statuary with its force.

Will looked around the room. Everyone was staring at him and nodding, as if to add their voices to Vera's. A few faces soon turned toward Joseph, begging him to say something when it was not clear what needed to be said.

Joseph accepted the prompt. "If what you're saying is true,

Will, we cannot—I cannot—stand behind you." Will refocused his anger on Joseph.

"Don't you see, Will?" Jay said, quietly. "You're going down."

"No, Jay," Will said. "You're going down. Alone."

"There's a paper trail," Jay said.

"Come on," Will said, turning back toward everyone. "I've given this synagogue, this city, more than anyone. You're going to throw that all away?"

"You threw it away, Will," Harry said. "You've gone too far, and you can't weasel your way out of this."

"Watch me." Will walked out and slammed the door. The noise reverberated through the room. Shlomo reached for another cracker. Everyone else sat still.

Jay sat down on the step descending into the living room and exploded into a wail. The Beth Abraham executive board was silent, watching him. Vivian lowered herself next to him. She put a hand on his back. No niggun, just a very loud silence that invited all the heaviness and relief to settle between them.

"Jay, why—how did you end up here?" Vivian asked, softly.

He held his face in his hands. "Phoebe, my wife," Jay finally began, "she found the envelope you left. She's a prosecutor, you know. She made me explain everything. The debt. Will's orders and threats. I got too tired of lying. When I told Will what you found, he said he'd take care of it and that he was coming here tonight to get you fired and off our backs once and for all. Phoebe was listening and she made me...." He trailed off.

"Why did you—why did Will do it?" Harry said, in a quiet voice that did not sound much like his own.

Jay took a deep breath and evaded Harry's stare. "Riverside's in a lot of debt. We needed the deal on the Banks Street plot. We had lined up a big loan and a tax break from the city for it, along with all the permits, so we could get the loan early. And we figured we could get a twofer by securing the renovation deal, too. But there were deadlines and debts we had to pay. It all had to happen fast."

Joseph walked over and kneeled down. "You have to turn yourself in."

. . .

No one called the police. Jay agreed to give a full confession to the authorities the next day. He figured he would get a lighter sentence by offering dirt on Will, who had been bribing and threatening lots of people—government officials, union executives and so on—for years.

"How could one of our own do this?" Shlomo asked, after Jay left.

"I guess we need to go back to the drawing board for the land and the renovations," Harry said automatically, ignoring the question.

"What about the South Side CDC's mixed-income project?" Vera asked. "The proposal is already drawn up."

"We'll look into it," Harry said. "If all the numbers check out and the public incentives go through—clean public incentives—let's just do it. Let's sign the papers and put all of this behind us."

The rest of the group rose quickly, anxious to escape. Joseph, Harry and Vivian remained, knowing important things remained unsaid.

"It's all so hard to make sense of," Joseph added, standing in the open doorway as a night wind bellowed around them, lifting the knocker ever so lightly. "Everything still feels so unsteady."

"Just like the mishkan," Vivian said, remembering Joseph's comments at the gathering Vera hosted after the fire.

"Hmm. Yes, just like the mishkan." Joseph said. "I'm sorry for not trusting you, Vivian."

"I'm sorry too, Rabbi," Harry said, looking straight at Vivian for what seemed to her like the first time. "You have to under-stand, Will is like a brother to me."

Vivian inhaled. She felt a softness travel through her body, telling each part that it could rest now. She nodded in accep-tance, knowing this was not the time to probe, to keep fighting, to cut deeper. Everything, everyone, was too tender.

As Vivian and Joseph strolled past a bed of Black-eyed Susans toward the street, Joseph stopped and turned to her.

"There's one more thing," he said. He inhaled deeply. "We have to set things right with Raymond."

FORTY-SEVEN

THE WEEKS RESIDENCE was brimming with glossy yard
signs and volunteers in homemade t-shirts. Mac, Greg and
a volunteer named Diane were staring at a map of their neighborhood when the phone rang. It kept ringing as Mac traced
the familiar streets, feeling his excitement build as he marked
the canvassing routes they had planned for the day.

"You going to get that?" Diane asked, and he pulled himself
away to walk to the kitchen phone. It was his pop's old boss,
Rabbi Joseph Glass. Mac couldn't remember him ever calling
before.

"He's at work. His new job, at the Garland Building downtown," Mac told Joseph, who had asked to speak to Raymond.

Mac paced as far as the phone cord would allow, peeking at the progress Greg and Diane were making.

"Will you tell him to call me when he has a chance?" Joseph said.

"Sure."

"Mac, do you remember me?" Joseph asked. "I know it's been a while, but I certainly remember you."

Mac smiled. "Of course. Your son Jake used to play with me when I was waiting for my dad to finish up work. Your synagogue was perfect for hide-and-seek."

Joseph laughed. "I'm sorry about what happened to you, Mac," he said.

"Thank you."

. . .

Joseph waited all week for Raymond to call back, but he never did. In the meantime, he heard from Chief Thicke: Jay had turned himself in and admitted everything. Now Will was suing Jay for slander and had left town on another so-called business trip.

The broken shards scattered around Joseph overwhelmed him: The damaged building. Will's betrayal. Gleeful comments about the fire that antisemites continued to post online, on websites he now knew about. The uncertainty of the future. It made him crave something that felt like repair.

So he drove downtown. On a bench outside the bland office complex, he waited for Raymond's shift to end. He stared at the sunset above the parking lot, trying to catch the sky changing colors, as he had with Jake when he was a boy. Sitting upright, Joseph fell into a shallow sleep.

"Rabbi?" a familiar voice said, startling him awake.

"I've been calling," Joseph said, rising from the bench.

"I know," Raymond said.

"Raymond, I'm so sorry that any of us ever suspected you." Joseph tried to remember what he had rehearsed on his drive over. "Will Gould started the fire. Well, to be accurate, Will ordered someone else to start the fire."

Raymond didn't seem to react.

"I've been thinking a lot about all this," Joseph continued. "We can't just let you leave the way you did." Joseph paused, and looked down at his hands, folding them in and out of each other, an anxious tic he had established years ago.

"Will you come back?" he asked.

"I don't know," Raymond said, sighing and rubbing both sides of his mouth. "I don't know if that's a possibility."

"I get it, Raymond. Well, I would like to get it. What I do know for sure is that we need you, and we would promote you. A raise and a new title, Director of Building Operations."

Raymond looked back toward the Garland Building. "I'll think about it."

"Okay. Give me a call to talk about details, if you'd like." Joseph nodded at Raymond, and he turned to leave.

"Hey, Rabbi," Raymond said, and Joseph spun back around.

"There's a big city council meeting coming up this Thursday. Mac is going to speak about moving public money away from the police department. They're trying to get a good group together to go. You know, a *diverse* group," Raymond said, motioning quotation marks. "Maybe you could come."

The invitation warmed something inside of Joseph, as if Raymond were talking about a Shabbat dinner instead of a municipal budget hearing.

"I'll try to be there. I'd like to help Mac," he said, aware and ashamed of his tendency to answer questions without making commitments.

"This is your chance, Rabbi," Raymond said.

"I'll try." Joseph reached out his hand. "Thanks for everything, Raymond," he said, not knowing exactly what everything contained.

Raymond stretched out his hand and shook Joseph's.

FORTY-EIGHT

RAYMOND WAS SQUISHED between a cluster of clergy and a portrait gallery of very old, very dead White men. Several ministers were wearing collars. Joseph and Vivian were piled in on the periphery, the ever-present kippa on Joseph's bald head being the closest thing they had to clergy garb. Raymond had puzzled over this plenty during his early years at Beth Abraham: How *was* it attached? The rabbi didn't use the clips others did, nor, to be frank, did he possess any hair that it could be clipped to. A miniature suction cup? A dab of rubber cement? Or did one spend years in seminary mastering this particular skill?

Letting the mystery lie, Raymond refocused on the room around him. He had never attended a city council hearing before. In the past, he had always suspected that—no matter how democratic city leadership claimed to be, no matter how doggedly his father insisted that every voice mattered—by the time members of the public were invited to comment, the deck had already been stacked...at tables and in rooms much smaller than Providence's city council chamber.

Councilor Clarissa Fox, the newly installed chair of the Finance Committee, was running the hearing. Mac had told Raymond that these were usually unremarkable events, with little media attention and low attendance; Raymond wasn't the only cynical one in Providence. Yet today, the room was packed, and Councilwoman Fox took control of the unusual crowd. She offered a warm welcome then listened intently as each testifier spoke. She registered a level of attentiveness that Raymond would not have expected from an elected official. He found himself letting his curiosity overtake his distrust.

Mac had been telling Raymond and Sheila about Councilwoman Fox. "The very first Black city councilor to chair the finance committee," he kept saying. By the end of the week, Raymond was reciting it along with him—rolling his eyes at Mac, but feeling his heart warm, too. Frequently having two opposing feelings about your child, Raymond had noticed, was part of parenting a teenager. Exasperation and devotion. Fear and excitement.

"Mr. Mac Weeks," Fox announced. Raymond shifted to the left for the clearest view. He was far more interested than he had expected to be, and more nervous, too. He watched his son approach the front of the room.

In the testifier's seat, Mac leaned toward the microphone. He got too close, and sharp feedback from the sound system jolted the crowd.

"Sorry about that, sorry," he said. Then he took a deep breath, cleared his throat, looked down at his notes and began. He described his recent harassment by the police, and Raymond listened to the familiar details. But then Mac continued. The time a slow-moving police car followed him, block after block, as he walked home alone from a friend's house. The time he watched two cops brutally question his cousin for a robbery whose suspect was a foot shorter. Parts of these stories were new to Raymond. He tried to remember if he had done the same with his parents, if he had held back details to ease their worry.

Now Mac was describing a time when he was little, riding home from his dad's work in the back seat, and Raymond was pulled over, because he was Black and they were on the east side of town.

Hearing Mac recount the story made him feel...Raymond couldn't even name it. His whole body tensed up, like he couldn't move.

In his mind, Raymond supplied the second part of the story: an impromptu trip to Toys "R" Us afterward, when he told Mac to pick out any toy he wanted. At first Mac was hesitant, but then he ran over to a Star Wars Lego set. The completed Lego Millennium Falcon spaceship was still in their basement somewhere. He had hoped that would be Mac's memory of the day.

Raymond caught Joseph's eyes on him. They were wide and seemed sad, helpless. Raymond looked away, wondering if he was reading the situation correctly: that what Joseph was hearing surprised him. Raymond turned back to Mac.

"You can't train away what has been engrained for years, decades, centuries. Change can only happen if the police get off our backs and off our blocks. And if city money is used to actually invest in Black lives and not Black deaths."

Mac got up and returned to his group. They doted and patted him down as if he had just crossed home plate. He looked for his dad over the sea of people, and Raymond nodded shyly at him. He was thinking of the lineage that Mac was a part of. Sheila had so wanted to be here, and Raymond rehearsed how he would describe the scene to her after work tonight. *Invest in Black Lives and not Black deaths.*

Councilwoman Fox called up Mac's friend Freddie to testify next, and Raymond relaxed into a daydream starring her and a future Mayor Alex Santiago. They would sit at ornate desks, crunch numbers, climb up on a dais, tell people what to do, overturn anything that didn't make sense, run circles around the likes of Cal Thicke.

Speak of the devil. Through the side entrance, Chief Thicke walked in. He waited for a Freddie to finish testifying, then headed straight to the microphone. The councilwoman introduced him as he sat down.

"Sorry to be late. There was, uh, an incident." Thicke promised internal investigations of officers who repeatedly used excessive force, then he continued with some platitudes about ensuring that the city's commitment to the department is an investment in everyone's safety.

People in the crowd hissed under their breath as Thicke spoke, and Councilwoman Fox interrupted a few times to remind attendees to be quiet and respectful. But it seemed to Raymond that she began waiting longer before her interjections. And though he wasn't one hundred percent sure, he thought he caught her hissing, too, when Thicke mentioned a monetary bonus for officers completing anti-bias training. Raymond controlled his emotions by upgrading his fantasy to a Mayor Fox presiding over Chief Thicke's last day on the job.

The hearing was drawing to a close. Alex Santiago, the last speaker, shared stories from other cities where funding for police had been successfully reallocated. As he listed types of services that had received much-needed influxes of cash—health clinics, daycares, subsidized housing, post-incarceration job training, harm-reduction programs to treat addiction, a crisis hotline especially for mental-health emergencies, and more—people cheered for their personal favorites. "We can, and we will, invest in Black lives, not Black deaths," he finished.

It was over. As well as he could in the crowd, Raymond stretched out his aching back. He heard someone call his name, and he twisted to find the speaker. It was Joseph.

"Thank you for the invitation," Joseph said. "What a son you've got. He's quite a speaker." They shook hands, and Vivian peeked out from behind Joseph to greet Raymond with a nod. Suddenly Joseph's expression changed. Raymond saw that

Chief Thicke had stopped alongside him. He watched Thicke and Joseph lock eyes.

"I thought you understood the importance of law enforcement, of...of security," Thicke said, neglecting the usual pleasantries. "You, of all people."

Joseph looked like he was going to say something in response, but Thicke abruptly turned away and pushed through a group of people on his route toward the exit.

Mac made his way over, redirecting Raymond's attention. A few minutes later, after congratulating his son, Raymond saw out of the corner of his eye that Vivian and Joseph were leaving. In the crush of people, Joseph bumped into someone, which knocked off his kippa. He caught it as it fell and returned it to its place.

FORTY-NINE

O UTSIDE OF VIVIAN'S door, Karla fidgeted with her bor-
rowed key. It was one a.m., the threshold between today
and tomorrow, on the night before the primary election. She
entered the apartment, tiptoeing through the living room and
into the dark of the bedroom.

At the foot of the bed in which Vivian was already asleep,
Karla saw the silhouette of a folded pair of pajamas. She fum-
bled quietly to put them on and curled up next to Vivian, whose
eyes opened. Vivian sleepily kissed Karla's shoulder and nuzzled
into the nook of her neck.

Karla laid awake in the dark, replaying the campaign in
her head. All the blunders. All the times Mike, the team, she,

came up short. She thought about what might be next. Maybe she had a shot at a job in the new administration, regardless of who won. All she was certain of was that she would have to start again. Again. That's how campaign life worked. And it was getting exhausting. She fell asleep in Vivian's arms for a fitful three-hour nap.

At six a.m. on Primary Day, as the sun was rising, Karla bought the standard coffee and doughnuts for the volunteers gathered at headquarters, starting their morning shift. She organized piles of door hangers, leaflets and stickers, labeling them with the names of streets in key neighborhoods. The stacks felt heavier than they had before, and even the volunteers who had stuck with the campaign this far accepted them with only rote enthusiasm.

After McCann's collapse, his shrinking base consisted primarily of the unions, which remained loyal to him, and the developers, who decided that they were not going to get anything from Alex Santiago or Margaret Heath. It was too late for either constituency to shift course. Beyond them, though, McCann held little appeal. Heath had picked up much of the support hemorrhaging from his campaign; she was the new frontrunner. Alex Santiago's profile had risen, too, as he stayed in the headlines.

Karla spent the rest of Primary Day driving around Providence, restocking materials in different neighborhoods, slow and uninspired. *This is how it goes,* she thought. *You sign your life over for a few months to one person, the idea of what they might be able to do, and you hope for the best.* She was proud of the positions she had helped craft for McCann—on development, on education. But he was not the politician, the person, she had thought he was. He deserved to lose.

At every stop she made, Karla thanked each volunteer she saw. They were handing out materials and reminding passersby to vote, calling and texting constituents. Yet she could not help noticing the buoyancy of the other campaigns' volunteers, zipping around town with the recognizable energy of people who believed in what they were doing.

Outside of Brownfield Elementary School on the South Side, Karla noticed a group of young volunteers for Santiago. They were pointing people toward the poll site and chatting them up as if they knew each voter personally. Meanwhile, the Heath team was everywhere: in smiling clumps 50 feet from every poll site; on the streets, door-knocking and leaving shiny door hangers; in cars, giving seniors lifts to the polls.

When the workday was over and the lines were at their longest, Karla found herself at the VFW post near Main Street. Vivian had texted that she was making her way there to vote, and Karla knew seeing her would be the boost of energy she needed to get through the rest of the day.

Approaching the poll site, she saw Vivian standing in line with Heather and her husband, Paul. As Karla walked up to them, Heather was showing off a 'Vote Heath Today!' sticker on her t-shirt. She caught sight of Karla and froze, looking guilty.

"It's okay," Karla said. "I know."

Vivian hugged and kissed her. "It's almost over, baby. And then we will go get all the beer you want." It was nice to have something else to think about for a moment.

Karla excused herself to find her volunteers. By the time she finished checking in with them, Vivian was close to the front of the line. Karla could see her chatting with the poll workers stationed outside the doors of the VFW. It seemed like she knew them. Perhaps they were congregants?

The race was called a few hours after polls closed. When Channel Seven broke the news, Karla was back at McCann headquarters with Mike and the team. Margaret Heath had won the Democratic primary with 51% of the vote. With no Republican challenger, she would officially become mayor the following month. Alex Santiago had finished second with 29%, while Mike McCann's well-funded campaign accounted for an abysmal 19%.

The loss was expected. The people had spoken. But the margin of victory was a surprise. Karla took a deep breath and surveyed the room. The torn yard signs reading "McCann Can!", the flyers and coffee cups strewn about, which under different circumstances might have appeared to be the vestiges of a hard-won victory, instead made it feel like a crime scene.

Karla, the rest of the staff, and the few remaining volunteers began cleaning up. Meanwhile Mike scowled on the office couch, glaring at the results on TV and the consolation texts on his phone. Seeing him stationary while others worked, Karla was overcome by frustration. She approached Mike and handed him her trash bag, which felt like it was all that remained of the last three months. "This time, you clean it up," she said.

Karla walked out of the building and into the moonlight.

FIFTY

I N THE SUMMER HEAT of First Parish's un-airconditioned auditorium, sixty-plus members of Beth Abraham pored over sheets of numbers and graphs, speaking loudly to drown out the fans.

The synagogue board and the South Side CDC had finalized a proposal for development of the vacant plot. In an hour, the congregation would be voting on it.

At the front of the room, several people prepared to make presentations and take questions. There was Bree Parker, the CDC's project manager; Vera and Joel, representing the board; Harry and Joseph, on behalf of the executive team; and

Raymond Weeks, Beth Abraham's new Director of Building Operations.

Raymond had negotiated the conditions of his reinstallation in a private meeting with Joseph. Vivian knew that a raise was part of his promotion, along with a real office and a part-time assistant. Finally, he had also asked for, and received, an honest apology from Harry in the presence of the two rabbis.

Bree climbed onstage first, firing up a PowerPoint. They would build 34 new units, 22 of which would be affordable. Lower-income residents would have the option to buy their units, along with a share of the collective amenities, through a special mortgage program. Bree detailed the tax break the project would receive under Mayor Heath's administration.

"We at South Side CDC will stay in close contact with the city to strategize about how this development fits into broader plans for equitable resource distribution," she said, "working with the newly formed Office of Economic and Racial Equity through our liaison there, Alex Santiago." She motioned to the back of the room where Alex gave a wave and a smile.

Vivian heard Sally and Farah cheering. Alex had endeared himself to them a week earlier when he helped facilitate a training for the synagogue's newly formed Community Safety Team. Team members would soon replace police officers for smaller gatherings and events.

Vera and Joel went next, with Joel proudly announcing that nine of the units would be set aside for local seniors.

Then Raymond got onstage, laying out the expected timeline of construction and explaining how each stage would impact use of the original building.

Sitting in the front row of folding chairs, handling the photocopy of the proposal as though it were a holy text, Vivian looked around her. There were Sally and Farah; Lisa, who had snuck in from her office down the hall to kiss Bree; Tamar Benayoun and her husband Perry; a couple of new members whom Vivian had yet to meet. She was far happier than she could ever remember feeling at a meeting with this many facts and figures.

After all the presentations and conversation, Harry, in his last act as President of Beth Abraham, called for a vote and guided the group through the motions. In the coming weeks, he would be handing over the reins to Vera. The proposal passed with ease.

FIFTY-ONE

A FTER THE FRIDAY night service ended, Vivian rounded up her dinner guests: Lisa and Bree, Ben and Flora.

Ben and Flora had been coming regularly since Vivian's Shavuot sermon. As Vivian had learned, Ben grew up having Shabbat dinner every week, but he had not yet been part of a Jewish community as an adult. Flora, who had converted a few years prior, had nudged Ben to explore Jewish ritual with her. Vivian had found herself gravitating toward them each time they came, learning more about what they were seeking.

She had also found that her congregants made exactly the type of nosy, assumptive comments to Flora that she had worried about.

"So, what's your…story?"

"You must be a fellow convert! I did it for marriage, too."

"You must be a member of First Parish. So nice that you stopped by."

Vivian had asked Flora what to do when she heard that happening, and Flora nodded thoughtfully. "Honestly, just break in and give me an out when I need one. Or help reset the conversation to something I'd be happy to discuss. The parsha…Star Wars…crocheting…."

"You mean, hover awkwardly and interrupt with something dorky? I can do that! I'm actually really good at that. We had a whole course on it in rabbinical school."

Flora laughed. "I've noticed, Rabbi."

. . .

Vivian and her guests walked in an easy cluster back to Vivian's apartment.

"I love going to services when I don't have to lead them," Lisa said.

"I know exactly what you mean," Vivian chuckled. "No matter how intellectually stimulating your sermons are, visiting your services is always so relaxing."

"Some of the tunes were different tonight," Flora observed, as they sidestepped a table of rowdy outdoor diners on the commercial strip of Providence's East Side.

"They were Sephardic. The chair of our ritual committee wants to expand our literacy," Vivian said. "What did you think?"

"Rabbi Glass didn't look too happy about it," Flora said in response.

"Oh, Joseph will survive. He has been dealing with a lot of changes lately," Vivian said. "He might look grumpy, but he's really coming around."

"You know, Vivian, this all turned out pretty well for you," Bree said. "With your new tunes, the construction project you wanted, and getting the old folks to pray in a church....Are you sure *you* didn't set the place on fire? Seems like the finger would have landed on you at some point."

"No one would have ever suspected it, right?" Vivian said, raising an eyebrow. Bree and Lisa laughed, but Ben and Flora held back.

"You know," Ben said, a tremor in his voice, "Last week, someone tied to a white supremacist group tried to blow up a synagogue a few blocks from my parents' house. No one was inside at the time, thankfully. But there was a lot of damage."

Vivian's steps grew heavier. She remembered seeing that news story on her phone and scrolling past it, willing herself onto the next story, convincing herself that *It* wasn't getting worse. As they rounded onto her block, she tried to open her mouth, to comfort Ben, to acknowledge his reality, her reality, her people's reality. But no words came out.

Bree saved her. "I'm so sorry to hear that," she said.

"There are just so many battles for us to fight," Lisa added, meeting Ben's eyes, putting her arm around Vivian.

. . .

They entered the apartment, still unsteadied by Ben's disclosure. A strong and confusing smell overwhelmed Vivian: delicious, then familiar, then totally foreign.

"Is someone making fried chicken?" Bree asked, clapping her hands.

As they walked into the kitchen to investigate, the stresses of the outside world dissipated in the warm light of Shabbat dinner preparation. Karla was standing over the stove, catching up with Heather and Paul, who was holding a sleepy newborn in what looked like a kangaroo pouch. And Karla, wearing an apron over her work clothes, was most definitely frying chicken. She had come straight from City Hall, where she had been hired in the Office of Environmental Affairs to implement climate adaptation projects.

"I thought you were *roasting* it," Vivian said, speaking directly to the cast-iron pan, unable to tear her eyes away from the golden flakes forming on the chicken pieces.

Karla leaned over and kissed her cheek. "Now you can eat it to honor Shabbat, instead of sneaking around."

"We heard about your fried chicken rule," Heather said. "I'm so glad we get to experience this momentous occasion with you."

Vivian let out a deep, grateful sigh. "This is the most momentous thing that has happened to me in a *very* long time."

Karla folded her arms, still holding the greasy spatula, and looked back at Vivian. "Baby, that can't possibly be true."

"Fine, but it's in the top five," she said. They all cracked up.

"All right, folks. Carry this stuff to the table, and let's eat!" Vivian ordered.

The rest of the group made their way out of the kitchen, introducing themselves to those they had not met yet. Vivian stayed back for a moment. She pressed her body against Karla's and kissed her, whispering, "I love you, Karla."

Karla squeezed her hand and kissed Vivian hungrily, as if to say it back.

ACKNOWLEDGMENTS

I N THE SUMMER of 2017, at a library sale in a small beach town in Massachusetts, I fortuitously stumbled upon a collection of mystery novels from the Rabbi Small series, the first of which were written in the 1960s. Once I started *Friday The Rabbi Slept Late*, I was hooked.

Throughout the series, the author, Harry Kemelman, used the genre of mystery and the contemporary milieu of a New England Conservative synagogue to comment on the dynamics of the American Jewish community at the time. (He had a real bone to pick with its assimilationist tendencies.) As I devoured the first few books, it became clear to me: an updated version was needed for *this* moment, one that would capture the formations and evolutions going on in Jewish communities across the U.S. today.

I had never written fiction before, but building off of the foundation set by Kemelman, I started to dream up scenes of a new young rabbi: queer; female; someone who must negotiate how to do right by her congregation and, simultaneously, the world beyond its four walls.

Vivian Green is a composite of handfuls of amazing women I know. Her processes of discovery, resistance and growth feel so familiar. It is impossible to capture all of the influences, all of the wisdom, all of the sources of strength and struggle in this story. But here is some of the gratitude I hold in my heart.

To the friends and family who took the time to read early drafts and offer feedback, loving critique, and encouragement. To Shahar Colt, Aliza Levine, Becca Thal, Talie Lewis, Yoella Epstein, Ora Weiss, Helen Bennett and Rachel Jacobson.

To my colleagues and collaborators through my work at the Jewish Community Relations Council of Greater Boston, along with the many clergy and leaders whom I have fought alongside in service of some of the same goals that Vivian and her allies seek. And to the organizers and thinkers who have developed a clear-eyed narrative of antisemitism—one that chooses solidarity over isolation—which has deeply informed my work and this book.

To the Hadar Institute for financial support through the alumni microgrant program.

To Anna Schnur-Fishman, my fantastic and astute editor who sharpened this novel and its characters in countless ways (and taught me a whole cannon of grammar rules I failed to learn in Jewish day school). To Brian Phillips whose cover (an homage to Kemelman's) and interior design really made it shine. And to my superb all-around hype woman/book publicist, Jenna Pollock.

Lastly, to my ever-supportive family. Specifically, to my mom, Sunnie, for being the first iteration of Rabbi Vivian. And to my wife, Liz, who has been a phenomenal and encouraging partner, and maybe even a better first editor.

I am deeply grateful to you all for helping me bring this book into being!

9 781792 356520